The Scenario

By

Psoemetry

&

The Ebony Poet

©2011 Safe Haven Publishing Company, First Edition

Safe Haven Publishing Company

ISBN-13: 978-0615503387
(Safe Haven Publishing Company)

ISBN-10: 0615503381

FIRST PRINTING
FIRST EDITION

Cover Art Design by The1Essence

I would like to dedicate this book to dreamers everywhere who have found a special place on this little thing we call "The Internet" For writers and spoken word artists everywhere and to special love. Lift your glasses up and fill your imaginations to the brim. Savor the flavor of life....add the coolness of expectations (shaken not stirred) then sip, never drink, until you are full. Enjoy!

~*Psoemetry*

FORWARD

By

The1Essence

Words cannot express my joy and honor to work with such a talented Artist. Psoemetry is not only a Poet, accomplished Spoken Word Artist but, now she adds Author to her growing list of creative achievements and, I am proud to call her a close friend and confidant.

From the moment I heard her spoken word track, "Who Drank My Kool Aid", I was hooked on Psoemetry! Shortly thereafter I had the opportunity to interview her about her artistic endeavors and her volunteer work around the Metro Atlanta aiding the homeless and, I knew I had a dear friend for life.

To me Psoemetry personifies the soulful, Spiritual, earthly embodiment that her name encompasses. There is nothing she does that comes without deep consideration of all who may encounter her work nor, is there anything she does that does not have a meaning.

I worked with Psoemetry on the publication of "The Scenario" from beginning to end. Each email, phone conversation or text message concerning this publication that we shared produced a literary work of art that can be enjoyed by all!

There are moments when I laughed, cried or even became angry with certain characters in this book. An Author who can invite you into the lives of their character and submerge you completely in their creation from start to finish has truly created a work of art worthy of purchasing.

But, don't take my word for it. As you read the novel, take the time to feel what Lauren and Troy are experiencing. Then visit Psoemetry's website and you will know exactly what I mean when I say: "You have just entered the Soul of Psoemetry"!

~The1Essence

About this book

Funny you should ask about how this book actually came about. There is a little truth to a little of it and much fiction to most of it. My name is Psoemetry and I am a writer, poet, spoken word artist and ba da ba da ba da.

The truth about this book is that I was actually on blackplanet.com when I met The Ebony Poet who is also a writer and an awesome poet…One of the best that I've met in a long time.

When E.P. and I met, the truth is that I WAS actually going to a concert to interview Anita Baker in Portsmouth Virginia in 2008. In my excitement in finding a new friend and fellow artist who was actually very, very good, I told him all about my quest to meet my favorite artist, Ms. Anita Baker!

Now I don't know why he decided to shoot me a scenario but it was quite a surprise. When I first saw it, I wasn't going to respond, but after reading over it a few times, the writer in me could not resist to send an answer back. I had no idea he'd send an answer to my answer.

E.P. was a very clever man. He wanted to keep the fun in what we were doing so he would make me wait until the following day to see what his response was.

I began sharing this with a few of my friends, R.M. Green, who is one of my publishers, Catherine Stewart, whom we lovingly call Kitty (who is the one who actually invited me to blackplanet.com in the first place. Thanks Kitty) and, Alexandria Coburn, one other friend I had met on line. (My mini me)

After a while this game I called *Scenario Tag* began to read like a real book! Originally I called it "The Concert." Once it was finished, I wrote another book around the inner book and named it, "The Scenario" after all, that's all it really was.

Let me also add that E.P., and I are just friends. He is married with children living in Texas and I am in a relationship with a wonderful man here in Atlanta, GA.

I hope you'll all enjoy this book. If there were a lesson to be learned here it would be to Love Deep, Love Real, and Embrace Life and Live like Today Is Your Last.

Enjoy this book and give it as a gift to your friends. You know the ones (smile) Again, thanks and true love to you all.

~*PSOEMETRY*

The Meeting

My name is Leigh. I'm a writer of sorts. Well, at least I try to be. I wanted a job in my field so, until I could actually get my own column at the Daily Press, I decided to get my foot in the door some way.

*Annnyy way,,*I can't remember exactly the day or the time it was when I met Mildred, but she was such a quiet spirit we immediately became friends. I wasn't really getting anywhere with the Daily Press, so I decided to do a little freelance writing. Maybe the Readers Digest would pick it up, or someone.

I drove down to Lincoln Park near the High Rise and decided to eat my sack lunch there. Maybe the birds would inspire me, or something. And.....that's when I met *her*. She told me her name was Mildred but, her friends called her 'Millie'.

"I could have been a Millie Jackson." she said, almost chuckling. "Of course I am older than Millie Jackson, but I tell you something, I am surely every bit as sexy".

I knew then that Millie and I would hit it off just fine.

Millie was very handsome in spite of her years showing. She looked out across the water and sadness filled her eyes. I could tell by her gaze, that those old eyes had some stories to tell and, I wanted to listen.

Never in a million years could I have even begun to imagine just how wild her story would be.
"Well?" Millie looked at me. "You gonna get a pen and paper or you just gonna keep staring at me?"

I reached into my pocket. "Oh no, I use this."

I pulled out my mini tape recorder and showed her. She chuckled and shook her head.

"I use to be a writer once a very long time ago."

I was impressed; maybe that's what it was. Her spirit was that of, the spirit of a writer.

"Got my share of awards too," she continued.

Millie turned to face the high rise where the senior citizens lived in the east end of town.

"I've got some right up there."

Millie's eyes seemed to come alive as she motioned towards the old building. She tapped me on my shoulder.

"Come on up. Let me show you some things."

I grabbed my lunch and followed Millie across the park, the street and the cluttered parking lot to the entrance to the building. As we entered the high rise, my nose picked up the odor of stale urine. An older man stumbled past us then turned.

"Ma'am." he began, extending his hands. "Got some change?" I smiled at him.

"No, I'm sorry." I tried to pass him, but he firmly took hold of my arm anyway.

"You think I'm gon' drink it up don't cha'?" he asked. I gently pulled my arm away.

"No sir, I just don't have any change." His rough hands sounded like sand paper as he wiped his mouth.

"I'm jest hungry that's all." he insisted. Millie, who had walked on ahead of me, turned.

"Luther!" she said firmly. "Leave that woman alone! Go ask Eloise for some lunch if you're hungry. She'll feed you. It's fried chicken and corn bread today."

The gentleman stood there for a few seconds then headed for Eloise's apartment.

Millie smiled, "That's Luther Hargrove, he's harmless. Give him a drink and he'll be your best friend. Only thing is, the doctor said the drinks are slowly killing him. But I guess he feels sometimes death may be the lessor of the two evils." I walked to the elevator.

"And what's the other evil?" I asked her. She waved her arms to show me the area where we were.

"Living in this place, or the life he has."

I looked around at the building. As I reached to press the button that would instruct the elevator to take us up to her 6th floor, I noticed that Mildred had continued walking to the stairs.

Turning she called, "Come on baby. We're not taking the elevator." I was convinced she must be joking.

"What floor do you live on?"

She opened the door that lead to the stairs.

"Floor number 6, and if you want to make it alive, you'll come with me." She laughed this time. Her laughter was very pleasant. It sounded kind of like music.

"That old elevator will get you maybe halfway to your destination." she started. "The fire department will have to open the door to let you out....and that's if you aren't dropped back where you just came from!" "Then if you live, honey, you'll still have to walk. So, make it easy on yourself and let's walk."

I began to follow Millie. Once inside the stairwell, I looked up at the winding stairs that seemed to go on forever.

I thought to myself, "She has GOT to be kidding me!" But nope! She was very serious.

We climbed those stairs flight by flight. She took those steps like it was nothing. I could feel my heart begin to increase its rate and, I tried not to allow Millie to hear my breathing as it quickened. She waited patiently for me at the sixth floor as I came off the fourth floor and headed for the fifth. I found myself almost pulling myself along as I reached the start of the sixth floor steps. My legs ached as I ascended the final section of steps. And, finally I was face to face with Millie again.

Almost out of breath I asked her, "How do you do this every day?"

Once I cleared the doorway she closed the door. "It's because I do it every day that I can do it." she smiled. "My apartment is this way." We walked down the dark hallway to her apartment. She reached into her pocket for the keys.

"That's how I get my exercise." The door swung open and we stepped in.

Her place was very organized and clean, very clean. She began proudly showing me the literary awards she had won. She had tons of them. She picked up a beautiful glass trophy with a gold quill and scroll in the center.

"This is 'the last one I received before my Albert passed away." Her expression became sad and distant. She held the trophy close to her heart.

"The night I received this, Albert was supposed to be with me. We were running late so he told me to go ahead and he would meet me there." She placed the award back on the table.

"May I touch it?" I asked her. She nodded and continued.

"He never did show up. It was the most important time in my life. And he never showed up. I was so upset with him. He was the slowest man I ever knew, so unorganized that sometimes I didn't know if I was his mother or his wife."

I was holding the award now. It was the most beautiful literary award I had ever seen. Millie walked over to her window and began closing blinds.

"Later during the celebration I got a call from the hospital. I'd wondered why he was moving slower than usual that day. I was so caught up in myself that I didn't even notice that something was wrong. And he wouldn't tell me." She heaved a sigh and went into the kitchen. She returned with two bottles of water.

"The last thing he said was, 'I'm proud of you...nothing is going to mess up my baby's day today'" She handed me a bottle as the tears quietly welled up in her eyes.

"He was usually right about things but, not this time." I replaced the award back on the table and thanked Millie for the water.

"Are you alright?" She nodded and softly spoke.

"Now don't you mind these old tears honey. It's all I have that I can share with him." I sat back in my seat as she dried her eyes and smiled again.

"God knows I loved that man. If I had only known I would have rather have had him than that award." She paused for a moment, and then continued.

"We got the call from the hospital. I'm thankful that I got a chance to tell him good-bye. I put down my pen and pad that very night and didn't pick it up again for many years."

The water was refreshing. It had bits of slush in it and the almost freezing cold taste was welcomed by my throat. I noticed what appeared to be a manuscript on the coffee table near me. I picked it up.

"What's this? Is this something you're working on now?"

She smiled. "I didn't pick up a pen or paper again until recently". I looked at the papers neatly laid in a box.

"The Concert?" I read the cover sheet. "Millie, is this a manuscript?" She nodded and continued to drink her water. That's exciting. When will you submit it for publication?" She began rocking now.

"I can't submit it dear." I turned the first page over as if it were fragile.

Very carefully, I protested, "Sure you can. Just do it." Millie rose from her seat.

"I can't publish it because it's not all my work. Someone else helped me write it."

When I started to speak further, she raised her hand.

"Are you hungry? I'm hungry. I'll fix something for us to eat. It's getting late. I'd like you to stay over tonight if you don't mind. There are some things I'd like to share with you. That is, unless you have someplace you needed to be."

I had no place to be. I just did have a job. Freelance only paid upon delivery. I was good to go. She smiled and returned to the kitchen. As I heard the pots and pans begin to rattle, I looked at the manuscript on the table beside me. I read the cover again, "*The Concert*"; Interesting.

Sleep came very easy that night. I woke to the aroma of French toast cooking and eggs and bacon frying. The smell of fresh roasted coffee almost lifted me straight out of the bed. I tossed the covers back and leaped to the floor. Millie approached my doorway.

"Are you hungry Leigh?" She asked.

She was dressed very nicely. Every silver strand of hair was perfectly in place. She even smelled of Chantecaille. I recognized the fragrance from a gift I had gotten one year. I mean she really looked nice. I pulled the night clothes she loaned me around me.

"I'm starving, like Marvin"

She laughed that very friendly laugh of hers, "Then," she started tossing me a towel and wash cloth. "Jump in the shower. Breakfast will be ready by the time you come out." She didn't have to tell me twice.

The shower felt real good and the soft soaps she had were only the finest. I wondered how someone as classy as Millie was come to live in a place like this high rise. I mean, she looked like she had money. The furniture was expensive. A blind man could see that. With the shower over I quickly dressed.

She must have laundered my clothing while I slept. Upon return to my room, I found my bed made and the slight mess of mine all cleaned up. My plate was on the table ready for me to indulge. And indulge I did.

"So, tell me Millie." The food was past delicious. "What's your story?"

I watched her between bites. My recorder was on the table and running now. She sat down across from me.

"What would you like to know Leigh?" she softly asked as she began to eat her breakfast.

"Only what you want to tell me."

I looked at her to study her expression. She smiled slightly. I couldn't tell if it were because of the great food or some random thought that had crossed her mind. She continued to eat, saying nothing.

Not wanting my food to become cold, I continued eating as well. Finally she gathered up our dishes and we cleaned the kitchen. She placed any leftovers into a foam container and bagged them up. She went to the door and passed the bag to someone. I now understood why she had prepared so much.

"Come here dear." she spoke softly as she began showing me her computer. "This is where it all began."

I looked at the computer. I mean it was a nice computer and all...

"It's a nice computer Millie." I responded.

She put her frail hand on the computer and ran her fingers across the top of it.

"Oh no dear," she smiled. "This is far more than just a computer. This machine saved my life. It's almost like a best friend to me." I was confused now.

She walked over to her manuscript still on the table. She tapped the book with the tip of her finger a few times.

"Leigh, let's go for a walk."

I was looking at the computer now. "What?" I asked.

She repeated extending her hand, "Walk with me." I agreed and followed her out of the door and back to the park. We walked along the water front and she began her story.

"After my husband died some years ago, I went into a severe depression. I didn't want to live and I just quit writing. Finally my son came and took me to live with his family. He hoped to help me get my writing itch back by taking me to events. Nothing worked." Millie looked at me and smiled.

The wind blowing through her silver hair reminded me of clouds in the spring.

"I have a daughter who is also a writer. She came over some time later....in fact not too long ago I would say. And she took me to live with her." There was that chuckle again as if she knew a little secret she wasn't quite willing to share, at least not all of it.

"My baby girl, she was always so wild that one. She bought me my computer and told me she was not going to leave me alone until I wrote something. She even took me to an online group on something called BlackPlanet.com and helped me join this group for writers. 'Meet friends,' she said. 'Write,' she said. And then she left me alone looking at the page she had pulled up for me." Millie's eyes began to twinkle. She shook her head. The smile was somewhat girl like now.

"And that, my dear, was the beginning."

"I sat at that computer for a while, and my daughter, bless her heart, came back into the room. She leaned over my shoulder and created a profile for me. No picture, no real information, except that I was a writer. And oh yes, that I was a woman living in Newport News, Virginia. Then she left. That's when the message came."

I shifted in my seat, "And what message was that?" I asked her almost ready to yawn. She reached over to me and lightly pushed my shoulder.

"The message from him." She looked too tickled.

"Who? What him?" Millie was on her feet now walking. "Hold it and let me change tapes." I hurried behind her. Okay" I sang, "ready now."

Her pace was a little faster as we headed back to the high rise.

"The message on the computer; it simply said, 'nice weather we're having today isn't it? I didn't know what to say. So I just replied, having weather is always nice."

We had reached the building and the stairs, (not the stairs again!!!!) Up we went. First floor (Oh lord) Second floor (help me somebody) third, fourth, fifth, floor, (I'm gonna die) Sixth floor (whew) Oh man, I can't take too much of this.

Back inside the apartment Millie began to prepare lunch. She fixed our plates and continued.

"He asked me for my name but, I couldn't tell him my real name, soooooo," she burst into melodic laughter. "I told him that my name was Lauren. Then he said his name was Troy. We shared a few things with one another and then before I could do anything, there it was on the screen."

I asked, "There was what, Millie?" She waved her hands lightly through the air.

"The Concert". Now I was really confused.

"That whole book?" Millie shook her head.

"No. Not the whole book, just a scenario. I had to finish it. And it was spicy and, oh my dear, I said to myself, this must be a young man. But the excitement to write again was coming back. I could feel it in my blood. I couldn't let on I was almost 76 years old. So....I played along and I joined in on the game." Millie went into the living room and picked up the manuscript.

"Here" she pointed to the unpublished book. "This is where the story began. Go ahead....Read it." I cleared my throat and started.

When Troy Met Lauren

Lauren and I were meeting in Midtown Manhattan for an Anita Baker concert. We had been talking to each other online and we both loved Anita, so when the tickets fell into my hands, I thought it would be a perfect first date.

I parked in the lot across from Carnegie Hall and walked to the spot where we had agreed to meet. As I approached, I could see she was wearing a very sexy dress with an empire waist. It came just above her knees and showed some sexy legs.

Once we were seated, we chatted, getting to know each other better since we were now face to face. As I leaned over to talk to Lauren, I picked up a very nice fragrance and her hair had that just shampooed aroma, like coconut oil or something. Her makeup was light but accentuated all of her facial features.

Anita began her set by telling the audience that she had a special guest in the audience who had started a fan club on ning.com and would be interviewing her after the concert. The house lights were dimmed and the music started.

We wanted to stand in the aisles and dance to her music. We were swaying in rhythm. All of our favorite songs were hit and the mood turned completely romantic. As Lauren got more and more excited, the hem of her dress began to ride up her thighs and the view was magnificent.

Anita then did her special number, 'Sweet Love'. She was dressed in this long black dress that hid some of the curves of her body. The stage lights dimmed and she was backlit. The light went right through that dress and her shapely body was silhouetted. I lost it.

I became as hard as Superman's belt buckle as did all the men, and a good portion of the women in the audience. The bulge in the crotch of my slacks was very visible.

Lauren looked down, noticed it, smiled and said…
(To be continued by Lauren)

When Lauren Met Troy

I looked up from the book. Millie was actually blushing now. "Wow", I said a little embarrassed. "When you read this, what did you do?"

Millie took a seat across from me at the table as if she wanted to see my reaction to every word.

"What else could I do? Was I shocked? Yes I was. But for whatever reason, I just joined and continued the story. He would write some and then, I would write some and it went on for days. We played what I call, '*Scenario Tag*', and it was so much fun. Please continue."

I returned my eyes to the pages. I could feel my cheeks getting warm. Did she have to watch me like that? I continued to read…

"Is that a hammer in your pocket, or are you just happy to see me?" We laughed, but just a little. I smiled, "Dance with me Troy."

He reached out to me and gently held me, but not too closely. And we danced to Anita softly singing '*Angel*'. From the stage, Anita glanced in our direction. She extended her arms pointing towards us and softly said, "I see you two over there. I see you."

The audience began to clap and the room filled with approving '*ahhh's*.' Soon the song was over and so was the concert. As people started slowly leaving , I lightly touched my hair as if to readjust my curls.

"It's time for my interview." Troy stood up, being very gentlemanly. Avoiding his eyes I asked, "will you wait for me?"

His large hand cupped my chin and tilted my face towards his. As I looked into his eyes, they twinkled almost magically.

"I wouldn't have it any other way." He slowly leaned towards me, very, very slowly. My eyes almost closed as his lips almost met mine.

"Go get your interview" he whispered. I smiled shyly, gathered up my things and headed towards the awaiting security guard.

Once the interview had ended, and it went very well I might add, I returned to the stage area. I was redirected to the lounge where Troy patiently waited for me. He didn't see me as I stood there just watching. He looked so handsome and, so relaxed. Not once did he look down at his watch or pace as if I were taking too much time. Just then he looked up. He smiled and started towards me.

"Would you like something to eat?" He asked.

"I, I don't think..." I began.

He gently took my arm and tucked it securely under his. My hand took his arm and rested on his muscle.

"Maybe we can go out for some desert or something to drink or, some apple juice or tea?" He remembered that I didn't drink.

"How thoughtful", I thought. He pulled my arm closer to his. "I'd like that." I smiled.

We went to his car after he assured me that mine would be safe and we wouldn't be gone long.

He took me to a quaint spot that had romantically dimmed lights and very few guests. We drank apple juice under the moonlight and danced. Oh yes, we danced! And, I couldn't believe how closely I held onto him as if he were the last man on earth. Soon he pulled me so close to him I could feel his heart just pounding...or was that mine?

The last song played and the last guest was gone. He brushed back my hair from my eyes and smiled.

"Time to go Princess", he whispered.

Releasing him, (the Lord knows I didn't want to) we quietly left the Café and he returned me to my car as promised.

The air began to feel a little chilly so he rubbed my hands to warm them up before he left. He opened my door for me and as I started to get into my car, I felt his arm slip around my waist. He gently turned my body until I was facing his.

In a very deep raspy voice he asked, "Did you have a nice time?"

I felt myself swallow and a very high pitched answer came out. "Yes".

Where did that come from? I was so embarrassed. He moved closer.

"I'm glad, so did I", he told me.

I could feel his breath on my cheek. It was hot but refreshing.

"I, I had a very nice time Troy."

His eyes closed this time and he pulled me yet closer. My back began to slowly arch as he moved in closer and closer until this time our lips met. The explosive fire shot throughout my entire body and it was as if the earth trembled...(or was that me?) I felt his warm hands moving slowly up my back, touching my spine and, the shivers ohh, the shivers. His arms tightened around my shoulders and my arms found themselves like an ornament around his neck. A strong pulsation riveted through my body. He gave me a hug that was so warm and inviting. I opened my eyes to once again see his. He was smiling again. He opened my door wider now. I slipped behind the wheel and he kissed me again, quickly this time.

"Will I see you again?" He asked.

Since we were both free and unattached I smiled. "I wouldn't have it any other way."

He closed my door and watched me drive away.

I went back to my hotel room remembering just how well the night had gone. Was it a dream, or did it actually happen? I jumped into the shower and got ready for bed. I wanted to pamper myself so I put on my red silk teddy. I had ordered a bowl of ice cream that had not yet arrived. Sometimes room service was so slow. But then, it was late and they didn't have to do this for me. There was a knock on my door. FINALLY!!! I pulled my robe together and swung the door open.

"I thought you'd never get here." I chimed. And there stood Troy looking like a dream holding my ice cream.

"I told you I would see you again." he smiled. And see him again I did. (To be continued by Troy)…

I walked in with a bowl of fresh ice cream, two scoops, and a wicked smile. Lauren was surprised, but pleasantly so. Her suite was well appointed and had a sitting area in the first room with the bedroom through an inner door. The small love seat had a small coffee table in front of it so I sat the ice cream down and we sat side by side. Lauren leaned over and placed a kiss on my lips and she tasted oh so sweet.

"I'm glad you're here Troy" she said. "But let's set the rules before I have to hurt you." She took her spoon and drew a line through the ice cream bowl.

"This side is mine, and this side is yours"

I protested, "And just why is my side so much smaller than your side?"

"Uh, who ordered the ice cream?" she quizzed.

"But it's not fair" I howled.

Lauren took the spoon and redrew the line, this time making my portion smaller than before.

"Listen you, do you have any other questions or protests before I draw this line again?" she asked.

"Uh, no." I said. I decided to quit while behind. I was born at night, but it wasn't last night.

She smiled, "I thought you'd see it my way Troy"

We proceeded to eat from the bowl. The ice cream was delicious. Lauren turned on the television and tuned into some jazz on the Sirius Radio Station.

"Surely they have an Anita Baker station," I commented. Lauren did some searching and found a station that was playing Anita Baker...wow.

Lauren smiled, "Shall we dance again?" she asked. We did.

As I held her in my arms, our bodies seemed to fit. I had both of my arms wrapped around her body and my hands clasped around her waist while she extended her arms up and around my neck.

The kissing followed. Her tongue searched my mouth as did mine hers. When we stopped dancing and sat back on the love seat, she leaned into my shoulder and I put my arm around her. We talked, kissed, caressed and just enjoyed each other.

It was about 3 a.m. and we both were sleepy so we went into the bedroom. We lay on top of the covers, holding each other until we drifted off to sleep. When I woke up the next morning, I was still holding her with her head nestled on my chest.

She opened her eyes slightly and I said, "Wake up sleepy head", she smiled at me and said, "Good morning".

(To be continued by Lauren)

The Morning After

I stretched and reached quickly under my pillow. I retrieved the mint that had been placed there earlier and, popped it into my mouth. There will be no morning breath here. I noticed that he too had found the mint under his pillow.

I started to get up and he gently pulled me closer to him. The strap on my teddy slipped off my shoulder revealing my cleavage. He smiled as he fixed the strap and pulled me closer.

"How did you sleep last night?" he asked. I snuggled closer to him.

"Like a dream", I answered. "I dreamed of ice cream...lots of chocolate ice cream" He sat up.

"Really?" he said almost laughing.

"Yes really. I never joke about ice cream."

I playfully hit him in his chest. He grabbed my hand and held it to his heart. I continued.

"I was swimming in it and, it....was...soooooo cold." He lifted my hand to his lips and kissed my fingertips.

Troy asked, "Was it a good cold or a bad cold?"

I sat up a little resting on my elbows. His fingers found their way to my chin and slowly traced my body, down my neck and gently down my chest stopping at the top of the center of my breasts. He drew an imaginary circle and kissed me ever so lightly.

"As much as you love ice cream," he spoke softly, "I'll bet it was a good dream". He kissed my shoulders, first one then the other.

"Troy", I whispered.

"Shhhhhh" he responded.

"Troy" I started again.

"Shhhhh" he repeated.

Then he brushed my cheek with the back of his hand. His touch was electric.

"Would you like some breakfast?" he asked leaning across my body to pick up the phone. "You can have whatever you want."

He crossed my body again, this time kissing me quickly on my lips. Then he playfully winked.

"What EVER you want." he repeated. I sat up bouncing in bed like a child.

"Whatever I want?" I asked. He nodded. "Good then, I want a T-bone steak, no make that porterhouse. I want it covered with onions and mushrooms. On second thought, hold the onions. I want ketchup, not steak sauce. And ah, some home fries and.....let's see....some scrambled eggs, not too soft, not too hard and, a diet coke. Ha ha just kidding about the coke. I'll take a glass of water with lots of ice. Oh, and some grapes washed twice and layered in a bowl of ice, crushed not cubed." He was sitting up now.

"Daaaaang", he was looking at me almost in disbelief. "Are you serious?"

I slipped out of bed and stood before him.

"Troy, you said....anything" He began laughing.

"That I did Ren; that I did."

He dialed room service and ordered just what I asked for and something for him. I could not believe this man. Should I pinch myself now or later? I ran my fingers through my hair and stretched. Tilting my head to the side I took a good look at him lying there in my bed looking like a hot fudge sundae on a cool Monday morning.

"I'm going to take a shower while we wait for our breakfast, Troy". I spun around and grabbed my silk robe and headed for the shower.

(To be continued by Troy)

"Let's see, steak, porterhouse, catsup (ewwww) eggs, toast, etc., makes a good breakfast. I'll order some water for Ren and some orange juice for me."

The sounds of Anita Baker reverberate throughout the suite and the aromas are lifting my spirit. I imagined that Ren was now in the shower with hot sudsy water cascading off of her naked body. Mmmmmm. A few minutes later, she re-entered the room with a luxurious bath robe wrapped around her. It was a short robe going to about mid-thigh, surely an appetizing sight.

"I wanted to check up on you, "she said. "I didn't want you to steal the furniture while I was out of the room."

Eyeing her lustfully I said, "It ain't the furniture I'm likely to steal Lauren."

She pouted, "You naughty man."

I teased her, "Oh what big eyes you have" Not actually talking about her eyes.

"You must be a Q" she responded. "How can you tell?"

She moved closer, "Because your tongue is hanging out of your mouth."

"I'm wounded," I protested with my hand over my heart.

"Po thang" she replied. "I'm going to get dressed before the food arrives."

Lauren returned to the bedroom. When she emerged 15 minutes later, she was wearing some white sling backs and black capris pants that did a great job of hurrying her anatomy and highlighting her thighs and butt.

She had on a white shirt that was not tucked in and the first few buttons were not fastened, showing some cleavage and, a sexy black lace bra. She walked over to the sofa, straddled my legs, and sat down on me. Our lips met and this woman took control of me.

My tongue traced the outline of her lips while my hands pulled her closer to me. She was perched on top of me and my aroused manhood was pushing at her bottom. The kisses deepened and I felt her tongue in my mouth. Probing, searching, tasting and I eagerly returned the favor.

The more I kissed her, the more I wanted to kiss her. I kissed her face, her neck and trail kissed down her neck until I reached the v between her breasts. Her soft moans only encouraged me further as she grasped the back of my head and pulled it between her breasts.

I kissed, licked and sucked what was available until I could get my hands between us to undo buttons. I had one button left to undo when the knock came on the door.

Dang! It was room service. I was already getting fed what I wanted and needed. Perhaps I could just send them away?

"Why don't we send them away?" I asked.

"Negro please!" was her quick reply. "You are going to feed me after trying to eat most of my ice cream last night."

The room service guy came in and put the food on the table and set everything out. The food was delicious and the steaks were cooked to perfection. We talked about a variety of things while we ate, including Anita Baker, writing, poetry, and Ren's CD.

At times she fed me and I fed her. Sometimes we kissed over the table. She was eating a piece of toast when a small section broke off and fell between her breasts.

"Let me help you with that," I said.

"Of course" was her reply.

"Come here," I beckoned.

She came around the table and straddled my lap again presenting her chest to me. I took a dive for the barrier reef immediately with my tongue searching between the twins.

She started undoing her remaining buttons to accommodate my adventures. Finally, the clasps of the bra demanded to be released and they were. Her nipples were now swollen with desire and it was like sucking a small grape into my mouth.

"Is this your desert?" she teasingly asked.

"Nawwwww," I responded. "This is my main course." She put her hands behind my head again and...

(To be continued by Lauren)

I felt my voice becoming husky. This man was so deep into my chest it seemed he'd enter my body at any second.

"Troy" my breathing was getting deeper.

"Yeah babe?," his voice was muffled

"Troy," I panted. He felt soooo good.

"Yeah babe?" he was breathing fast and deep now as well.

I felt my body begin to surrender and I struggled beneath the bonds of passion.

"Take me...." then my cell phone alarm went off..

"Take you?" he was very excited now. "Take you? Are you ready for me to take you to..."

I leaped to my feet and shouted, "To the airport! What time is it?"

His lips were still puckered and an expression blended with disbelief and confusion crossed his face. He shook himself.

"Take you to the airport? What the?"

I quickly buttoned my blouse. "I'm so sorry baby, but I had totally forgotten about the concert."

He stood up looking as if Pinocchio had jumped into his pants and told the biggest lie he could ever think of.

"We just came from the concert last night. What concert are you talking about?"

I began looking for my keys and tossing things frantically into my suitcase. I had never dreamed that he would be such a delicious man, nor did I or could I ever have imagined that things would go this far.

"I have a concert in Atlanta tonight. I'm opening for Patti Labelle at the Fox Theater."

He shook his head and asked, "Now how could you forget something like that?"

I was frantic, what if I miss my plane and can't get out? I still had to return the rental car. I leaned my head back and closed my eyes, "STUPID, STUPID, STUPID!!!" I repeated.

Troy slowly came behind me. He put his big strong hands on either of my shoulders and began to gently but firmly massage. His voice was softer now.

"Don't worry about it. I'll take you to the airport and call someone to pick up the rental car. I'll take care of everything. Double check and make sure you have everything and you're not leaving anything behind. Do you have everything?"

I felt like crying. What will this man think of me now? I nodded and I could feel my bottom lip tighten. I blinked my eyes so I wouldn't cry. He picked up my suitcase and grabbed the keys to the room.

"Come on Princess," he whispered.

Pinocchio was at full mass now. He must be so angry with me. My voice cracked as we walked into the office.

"Troy are you angry with me?"

He didn't look at me but asked, "For what?" I lowered my eyes. Turning, he looked at me and asked again, "for what?" I motioned towards his pants.

"You know," I softly answered.

He laughed slightly, "Oh slugger there? Nah, it's just one of them thangs baby gurl, what time is the show?" I felt so guilty. I didn't mean to tease him.

"The doors open at 7 and the show starts at 8."

He checked me out and paid for the room. I was surprised. 'Is he for real?' I thought. I gave him the keys to my rental and he opened the door for me. We had to hurry so I wouldn't miss my flight.

Troy started the car and winked at me. "Opening for Ms. Patti" he smiled and headed towards the airport. "My baby!" He seemed excited.

I half expected for him to lay me out, but he didn't. So why didn't I feel relieved? Soon we were at the gate and it was time to say, 'good-bye' I felt the tears falling now.

"When will I see you again?" I asked him. He gently wiped the tears from my eyes.

"I'm as close as your heart," he smiled.

I shook my head. "No really, when will I see you again?"

I repeated the question. I heard them call for my flight and he took my hand and kissed it.

"Go do Miss Patti proud."

As I walked away, I stopped to see if he were watching me...and he was gone. He didn't wait and my heart began to sink. What would have happened if I made love to him last night?

Sure we had been talking for some time during our long distance relationship...but we did only just actually meet. That would have been wrong. But, then the morning after, was that any more right? It didn't matter anyway since, I was leaving him behind.

I was safely on the plane now and heading back to Atlanta. The scene played over in my mind where Whitney Houston in *The Body Guard*, ran off the plane and back into the arms of that fine white man, Kevin Costner. But, this was real life and there would be no running off any planes into anybody's arms today.

Nope.....not today.

It didn't take long for the plane to land. Yet it seemed like hours. I had been crying, just a little. I pulled out my shades to cover any traces of tears so, when my son picked me up he would be none the wiser.

Once outside of the terminal I saw him. He was as handsome as he wanted to be. He waved and hurried to give me a hug and a great big kiss.

"Welcome home mommy" he sang. "How was Anita?"

I tried to smile. "As awesome as ever," I answered and, he began to just chatter away. I tried to listen but finally gave up.

When we reached our home, he was still talking. "Your manager said she would pick you up in about an hour. Ms. Labelle wants everyone there to do a dress rehearsal. It's going to be televised so she wants it to be right. Plus we have to set up your concession tables."

My heart hit the floor. "Televised? No one said it would be televised"! I was shocked. "I didn't know it would be televised." I repeated. My son leaped from the car and grabbed my luggage.

"Don't worry, be happy mom." he smiled. "But, you might want to hit the showers, you smell like men's cologne. You'll do great.....relax. You're the Psoemetris!"

As he hurried into the house I thought. "I know that little rascal did not just tell me to take a shower. I'd better go take a shower."

When we reached the Fox about an hour later, everyone was there. Patti looked so radiant. She had arranged for everyone to have a room at a nearby hotel. She didn't want anyone to be late. As a promotion, the hotel paid for it all, lucky for me.

I was handed my key to my room and given my wardrobe by my stylists. I was informed that my makeup artist would be over by 5:30 and, because of some technical problems, the dress rehearsal had been pushed back for two hours. My son had already left to go pick his girlfriend up.

"Two hours? What in the name of Charleston Blue was I going to do for two hours?"

Just then I heard a voice behind me...." I can think of a few things..."

It was Troy...

(To be continued by Troy)

Peachtree Street was very crowded and, the traffic was backed up even when I was exiting off l-20. I drove around a few cars and went through some yellow lights.

Having my friend Malcolm use his Piper Cub 2 seater to fly me to Atlanta had been a last minute inspiration. There was something about this woman that kept me enchanted and I intended to find out what it was.

Locating her was the next hurdle. I went to The Fox, asked for her and, was told her dress rehearsal would be delayed for two hours and that; she was probably at the hotel. She had told me she would be staying at the Georgian Terrace, so I went to the front desk. As I approached, there she was waiting on an elevator. She must have felt my presence because she turned around just as I was answering her question about what to do for the next two hours.

There was a street Cafe a block down from The Fox and we casually walked to it. The afternoon temperature was mild and there was a nice breeze blowing in from the northwest. We ordered coffee. I had cheesecake with mine and she had ice cream with hers as we sat and talked.

I told her about my childhood. It was important to me that this woman got to know me and I get to know her. Physically, she was alluring, sexy, and sensual and, I loved to touch her. I wanted to see the emotional, spiritual and mental side of her.

I told her about my beginnings in rural Arkansas and, about how my dad had left the family when I was two years old. How he had never provided for my support nor did he interact with us as a father.

He had lived about 10 miles away and the only time we saw him was when we went to see him. We would hitch a ride to his home, which was a country storefront, right after Church on Sundays.

Sometimes my mom would pack a box of food for us to take to him. She had taught us to love him no matter how he treated us. Many winters passed when we had little food to eat and, he never brought us anything to help. He told my mom that we would never amount to anything and, all of us became very successful. I only wished that he was still alive so I could walk up to him and say, "Look Dad, I made it!" I watched the struggles of a single mom and vowed that when I had children, I'd endure anything to stay with them and make sure they had a father present in the home.

I attended college in Arkansas and then, moved to New York when I graduated and, began working with one of the large computer companies where I was like a lost ball in high weeds but, I soon learned to adapt. I met many new friends and learned from them while they learned from me.

I started writing when I was 14 and stopped when I finished high school right after I told my freshman advisor that I wanted to be a writer.

He told me, "Son, writers often starve to death and Black writers are the first to starve. If you want to write, do it as a hobby and go into something that can feed you and your family. Write as a hobby." So I did.

I started back writing some 20 years later and met a friend online who encouraged my writing. Each time I wrote a poem, I would share it with her. Over the years, she collected those poems and had them typed up and put into a binder. She presented the collection to me as a birthday gift and, I was eternally grateful. I used that collection, to self-publish several chapbooks locally. I also remained active in church and in the community, sitting on several boards of community organizations. This conversation continued for an hour while we sipped coffee.

Occasionally Lauren would reach across the table and touch my hand or, give it a squeeze.

I suggested we get back to her room. She needed to at least get a few minutes of rest before returning to The Fox. We walked along, holding hands and occasionally bumping each other with our hips. I slowed down a bit, so she could get a step or two ahead. From that vantage point, I would watch her rear end.

When she walked, her hip action swayed her butt from side to side gently and, I felt a stirring in my groin. I think she realized what I was doing because she turned her head, looked over her shoulder, and smiled seductively.

When we got back to the hotel, we went to her room after checking for messages. As soon as we got inside, she tossed her purse on the sofa and pushed me against the door. In her heels, she stretched just a mite and her lips met mine. Gently and caressingly we stood there looking at each other breathing rapidly.

"Uh, I said, you needed some rest before going to the theatre, so why don't we continue this after the concert?" I asked panting.

She smiled, "Okay. Just remember, we have a date." I fixed my clothes and smiled back.

"I'm glad you mentioned that. I made late reservations for us at Mary Mac and, I'll get a room here on my way downstairs." We kissed again and held that kiss for five minutes while our tongues explored each other.

"See you at The Fox", she said. And with that, we kissed again and I walked out the door…

(To be continued by Lauren)

I could not believe this was happening. No man had ever pursued me like this before, ever. What made me so special? Just the thought of him made my entire body burn.

I decided to jump into the shower, cold this time. The cold water was a shock at first, but as my skin began to cool, I welcomed it. Tonight was a very big night for me. I had been making my rounds here and there to some of the smaller local spots presenting my soft spoken word poetry. Who would have ever thought that Tyler Perry would have brought Ms. Patti out to the Apache Cafe on that wonderful, "God Blessed" Thursday night?

I opened my mouth to receive the cool water on my tongue. Careful not to swallow, I just let it roll around in my mouth before setting it free. I closed my eyes and leaned against the wall waiting unsuccessfully for my insides to match my now chilled outsides. It wasn't about to happen. Even the thought of that man made my blood steam.

I heard a pounding on the door. Quickly I grabbed my towel and hurried out of the shower.

"Who's there?" I asked.

"Gurl, open up!" came the voice from the other side.

What time was it? How long had I been in the shower? I cracked the door.

"Gurl let me in". I stepped back from the door. "Put some clothes on, I ain't tryin ta see you naked honey." Sylvia swayed into the room with her makeup kit and towels draped over her arm.

"Nice place here. Is your hair wet? Let me see. Gurl, your hair is wet! I ain't got time to curl your hair tonight. Let me see, I'll think of another style for you tonight. You still naked? Gurrrl, get some clothes on before you catch a cold. You nervous? I'm nervous for you."

I began dressing as she grabbed her blow dryer and hooked it up.

"Come on now" she continued. "Day light's bumin'. Let me see what you're gonna wear tonight." I suddenly remembered why I always had Sylvia do my makeup and hair at the last possible moment. She just could not stop talking.

"Gurl that is sharp right there! I've got just the perfect colors to go with that. Awww sookie, sookie nah."

She talked too much, but was an absolute genius. She tied my hair back and went to work on my makeup. Then she did my hair. When she was finished I was so excited at what she had created.

"Sylvia!" I started. Grabbing her gear she smiled.

"I know, I know. I'm a genius. Now get dressed chile. You 'bout ta blow up!!!"

She slapped me a 'high five' and was gone as quickly as she had arrived. I put my outfit on for the concert, whispered a prayer and locked the door behind myself.

Troy was heavy on my mind and, I knew if I was going to get through this night I would have to stay focused. Once back stage, Ms. Patti gave me a big hug and told me how great I looked. She handed me a bottle of Pepto and smiled. She must have been reading my mind.

I took a huge swallow and handed it back to her. We quickly ran through the show then it was 'get ready time' as the crew called it. I could hear the audience as they began coming in. There were so many people.

When I saw my son I felt better. Then I saw Troy. What was he doing? I watched him walk up to the front row and pull his wallet out. The guy on the front row got up from his seat and took something from Troy and Troy sat in his seat. Front row center.

The lights began to flicker. My heart jumped. "I can do this." I assured myself.

All those people....wow. This can go either way. Then he caught my eye. He smiled and waved and gave me a hearty 'thumbs up'. I smiled and waved then caught the kiss he had thrown me. I laughed when Troy motioned that I looked hot.

A stage hand gently tapped my shoulders, "Places please" he said. Then he squeezed my shoulders and smiled. "Tear it up Ms. Storme."

I placed my hand over his and nodded. "Thank you Dave."

My act had begun to take the stage behind the curtain as the announcer took center stage. He welcomed everyone and thanked them for coming. Then he began to speak about me. I took my place behind the Mic. This was it.

I made up my mind that I would grab every bit of passion I was feeling for that man in the front row and throw it into my poetry for that evening. The curtain went up, the music began and the audience roared. I grabbed the mic and took control of the stage, the audience and my passion. I was in heaven and everyone in the house must have gone with me.

The night ended with Ms. Patti doing two encores followed by several standing ovations. I was too thrilled when I heard her call my name. The curtains went up and I reentered the stage. I took Ms. Patti's hand and we both bowed.

"Y'all get her CD's now you hear me?" she shouted.

How kind of her to encourage them to support me. The curtain closed just as it had opened, with me standing there in awe of it all.

I heard a small commotion on the other side of the curtain. When I pulled it back to look, there was my son, a security guard and Troy.

"It's alright Ed," I called. "They're with me."

I introduced my son to Troy and we talked for a little bit, then my son and his girlfriend left. Troy took my hand and, kissed me on the cheek.

"Good job" he smiled.

I said my good-bye's to everyone and of course introduced the man of my dreams to Patti Labelle. We then left for Mary Mac.

Holding hands we ate while few words were spoken. Occasionally Troy would caress my finger tips or lean over and gently kiss me on my lips. I stretched my leg towards him under the table and Troy instinctively grabbed my foot. He placed my foot in his lap and removed my shoe with one hand while he continued to eat with the other.

Troys touch on my foot was like magic. Those big hands were so graceful and soothing to the touch. I put the last spoonful of ice cream in my mouth and let it slide down my tongue, leaned back, closed my eyes and smiled. I didn't even know I was smiling. That's how good he was.

Troy gently tugged at my foot. "Let's go" he smiled.

He paid the bill and left a nice tip for our waitress. Then he extended his arm and I placed my 5'1 frame just under his heart. I felt so safe as he towered over me. I never knew he was so tall.

Once we reached my room, I handed Troy my keys. Opening the door for me, he lifted me into his arms and carried me over the threshold. I tossed my purse unto the table as we passed it. When we reached the bed, Troy pulled back the covers. Ever so gently he laid me down.

The look in his eyes was so intense…

(back to Troy)

"May I undress you?" I whispered.

"Do you really want to?" Ren asked.

"More than anything in the world" I responded. "I'm yours" she whispered.

I kissed Lauren long and hard. I inhaled the air the she exhaled. I slowly began to remove Rens' clothing, piece by piece. First her heels, then the dress that slid off her body aided by the silken panty hose. All of Lauren's undergarments matched and, were sensuous to the touch. Now she lay there in a matching bra, panties and, panty hose.

Lauren's hair was splayed over the pillow and she was smiling a contented smile. I stepped back a few paces and just took in the visuals. I could see her chest rise and fall and it matched the pulsing in my manhood.

As I stood there, I began to strip my clothing off. Lauren instructed me to wait so that she could do that herself. Lauren had me sit on the side of the bed while she removed my shoes and socks. I had already removed my jacket and left it in the other room. Ren removed my shirt and necktie and undid my belt buckle. From somewhere in the other room Anita Baker's, *Sweet Love* began coming out of the speakers.

Once Lauren removed my slacks, she pulled me up from the bed and we danced the dance of intimacy. My arousal nestled against her naval while her ample breasts pushed up against my upper torso. She had slipped her heels back on and it had pushed her pelvic into me and I loved the feeling.

Her fragrance was invading my brain as my heart raced. The silky feel of Lauren's pantyhose against my bare leg put my senses on overload. Occasionally she would raise one of her legs and caress my bare leg with her encased leg and my bulge would grow larger.

My arms went to Lauren's waist, and my hands dropped down to cup her butt. I caressed it, held it and, pulled her closer to me if that were possible.

Lauren surprised me by returning the favor. She wantonly caressed my butt and purred as she did it letting me know it was enjoyable. Our feet stopped moving and we stood there in the same place, moving our bodies to the music. It reminded me of when I was in high school and we had those Friday night dances in the gym.

We would stand in the middle of the floor or, more likely a darkened portion of the gym floor and dry grind. By the end of the evening, the boys often had juices running down their legs while the girls giggled and stuck their little pointed chests out because they realized they had that power over us.

Lauren and I stood there stroking each other going back and forth, back and forth. We went back to bed where Ren lay on her back as I stood on the side of the bed slowly removing her panty hose.

As I peeled the pantyhose off, each inch of skin I exposed seemed to call my name. My boxers were standing out like a tent and Ren was caressing me through the fabric. I undid her bra and lie down beside her and we cuddled, kissed and held each other close.

I was amazed at Lauren's full breasts and filled my hands with them. They were firm, yet soft and I wanted to make love to them. Lauren rolled on her side and draped her leg over mine and rested her head over my heart, listening to my heart going...'thump...thump...thump...thump'.

Lauren looked at me and said....

(To be continued by Lauren)

"I think I'm falling in love with you Troy." I whispered. Troy looked gently into my eyes while his hands carefully stroked my breasts. He kissed my eyelids and I could feel and hear his breathing deepen.

"I've never met anyone like you before."

My voice got quieter softer quivering I whispered "Troy what if "...Troy placed his finger tip across my lips and smiled. Tears filled his eyes.

"I fell in love with you the moment I laid my eyes on you."

I reached up to catch a tear that had gathered in the corner of his eye. I missed and it fell almost in slow motion and splashed on my chest, in a small curve of my breasts. Troy lowered his head slowly as other tears gathered in that special place and then he....he drank his tears from the well of my chest.

My skin began to tingle. I never wanted a man the way I wanted this man. I cradled his head and a sea of love welled up from so deep inside of me from a place I never knew it could ever be possible. Troy moved his mouth from the left then to the right and, I could feel the perspiration begin to surface on my face.

Looking up he ran his hands across my face. I smiled as his hands skillfully traveled across my body, not missing a single spot. Then, Troy touched me there...and there ...and.....there and, I loved it. My body begged for it and his body heard.

I closed my eyes and felt him hover over me. He ran his fingers through my hair and I could hear the music playing in the background. The music slowly began to get dimmer with each touch until, it vanished all together.

"WALK WITH ME"

Walk with me at dusk
over the sands of the beach nearby.
Walk with me as we listen to the sea,
and he surf coming back home.
Walk with me and hold my hand.
Let my fingertips caress your palms.
Feel the energy inside my body
aching to connect with yours.

Walk with me while I think thoughts
Of you while we lay there last night.
While you smiled and lay on my chest
listening to the sound of my heart beating.
Walk with me as we walk the surf
feeling the warm sea on our feet.
Feeling the sea breeze on our backs
and a salty taste in our mouths.

Walk with me as we pass lovers on blankets
listening to sounds of love being made.
The movements of love all around us.
With bodies entangled in the sand.
Walk with me once again this day.
Take my hand to your body.
Let me touch the places where you like
and think sweet thoughts of us entwined.

Walk with me darling,
Let my lips touch yours.
Make the tip of your tongue enter my soul.
I will inhale the air that you exhale.
Walk with me, be by my side.
My hand placed on your thigh

sensing your movement as you walk
with me at your side.

Walk with me in this dusty light
and let us pause to kiss
tracing the outline of your lips with my tongue.
Arms pulling you closer to me.
Walk with me as I feel your breasts
full and heaving against my body.
Nipples taut and pushing upward.
A quickening of the breath...it is time.

Walk with me and share your warmth
as your body prepares to surrender it's essence.
Surrounding me with your treasures of love
I slide my leg between your thighs.
Walk with me as we think of love
and lovemaking as we often do
walk with me and hold me close.
Enjoy the tender caresses I so eagerly give.

Walk with me so I can be
all that I am to you.
Share this night of love with me
and walk with me while I love you.
~© Ebony Poet

The Sweetness

As I suspended myself in midair over Ren's body, she smiled such a serene a seductive smile at me. With, Ms. Patti (Lauren named her bra's after her favorite singers) already off, Lauren's perky breasts beckoned me to come and devour.

On my knees at the foot of the bed, I removed Lauren's black pantyhose and her black lace high thigh cut panties. Slipping them over her rear end, then sliding them down her thighs, legs and off her feet, only served to arouse more an already engorged shaft.

I found my slacks where they had been discarded and removed a condom from my pocket. It was a natural feeling condom because I wanted to feel as much of Lauren as I possibly could.

"Here, let me do that" Lauren said as she took the packet from my fingers.

I stood on the side of the bed with my member at full attention. Lauren stroked it gently with her hands wrapped around it and I thought I was going to have an orgasm right in her hands.

Lauren sensed that and gave it a gentle squeeze and the need to cum left me. She rolled the condom on, admired her handiwork and then pulled me down onto the bed on top of her. We continued kissing like two high school teenagers.

While I kissed Ren's lips and sucked her nipples, my hand traveled the length of her body and found that inviting patch of hair. I ran my fingers through it until I found her nub, coaxed it out of its hood then, gently and slowly caressed it until it stood at attention. Ren's little man in the boat was alive and well.

Lauren reached down, grasped my sheathed tool and pulled it and me toward her wet center.

"Now" she whispered.

Lauren guided me inside of her and I watched her eyes roll back in her head when the full length of me entered. We started a slow, rhythmic stroke and soon harmonized it between us. Our bodies fit like a hand and glove.

I sucked Lauren's breasts and we made love. We continued stroking each other and the sounds of our wet lovemaking filled the room. Suddenly, Lauren rolled me off of her, mounted me and rode me.

I continued sucking her breasts as she rose and fell on my engorged shaft. Up, down, up, down, up, down, up, down. There seemed to be urgency in our stroking as if we could not get enough of each other.

Ren continued stroking and I was beginning to feel the fullness in my balls. She knew that and, soon started stroking faster. Lauren reached behind me, gently grasped my balls and caressed them. By this time the whole bed was moving to our rhythm and I literally could not get deep enough inside her.

Our breathing became labored, ragged, and urgent. I was calling her name but, I'm not sure what language I was speaking in because I could not understand what I was saying. Suddenly the stroking became frantic and Lauren gently squeezed my balls and I had a tremendous explosion.

While I was at the height of my increased, frantic, urgent stroking, Ren came with a flourish. I was stroking so hard that I was lifting us both off the bed. As I watched Lauren rise and fall on my ebony shaft, I noticed how wet I had become with her juices.

When Lauren came, a torrent was released and it mingled with my just released juices and we created a wet spot on the sheets as big as the Mississippi River. Lauren contracted the muscles of her center and milked my fluid from me. Then Lauren collapsed on me and we remained in that position with me still inside of her. As our bodies both cooled down and slowed down, I could feel Lauren pulse through my manhood and I loved the feeling.

Lauren rolled off me and curled against me. We kissed again then, she wanted to go take a shower.

"No." I gently told her. "I want you near me."

"But I smell" she started.

"Like sex...." I finished. "And that's how I want it."

I rolled Lauren over so her back was to me and she curled with her knees slightly drawn up. Lauren's butt pushed back to me, my arm over her body caressing a breast. We were touching from head to toe. We were spooning; the afterglow of love making. My shaft was nestled between her cheeks and it felt good leaving it there. We slept.

I CAN'T BELIEVE

I can't believe this man was so deep inside of me.
He touched my thighs with his hands;
they parted like the red sea.
Then he took a ride in me.....
So deep inside of me...
Oh this man.
Oh this man.

The music played softly on the radio.
He took my garments layer by layer
nice and slow.
Then the rodeo,
took me head to toe.
Oh this man.
Oh this man.

A beautiful silence. First it filled the air.
Beautiful music as he stroked my hair.
Then he touched me there...
chocolate everywhere!
Passion is building. I can feel the sound.
Oceans of motions....lay my body down.

Such an awesome sound
Soaring heaven bound.
I can't believe that I am so into you
Got me doing things thought I'd never do.
Made an art of me, and every part of me.
Oh my man, don't let me go...
Never let me go.
-Psoemetry

Afterglow

I opened my eyes. It was light outside. I rolled over and there was Troy, still holding me as if his life depended upon it. The sheets beneath us were damp and sticky. Carefully I slid from between his arms and out of the bed. I didn't want to wake Troy. What time was it? 11:00. Check out time was at 12 noon.

I ran my fingers through my hair. I always did that when I was a little on edge. What in the world did I do? I can't believe what happened had actually happened. Yet I didn't feel a bit guilty. Could it be that I actually did love Troy? I mean, he just took me like a cave man and rode me like ..oh my, gosh, and I actually liked it. I mean I reeeeealy liked it.

I walked to the showers, not bothering to grab my robe or any clothes. After all, Troy saw it all last night. Why try to hide anything now?

I shook my head again. Look at him. Look at him laying so peaceful in my bed sleeping as if he actually belonged there. I must be crazy or, mad or, something. I can't believe that we did what we did. And what's worse, I can't believe I wanted more.

The moment Troy touched me last night, every inhibition I ever held on to was gone. Like that, all gone. Gone like the vegetables I hated when I was a young girl.

I started the shower and looked at myself in the mirror. You're not a young kid anymore Lauren. You'd better pull yourself together on this one. Guard your heart and get prepared.

I stepped into the showers. The water flowing swiftly and streaming over my body felt so relaxing. Last night Troy worked muscles I didn't even know I had. Of course, don't think I didn't do a little sumpin sumpin to him too now. I had to smile at that.

I must have stayed in that shower for nearly an hour. I kept adjusting the water as it started to cool down to make it hot again.

I decided to wash my hair since I was in the mood for some *me time* in the shower. As I stepped out of the shower I could hear voices and someone leave the room. *That Troy*, He must have ordered breakfast. He's just too wonderful! I wondered if Troy remembered. I dried quickly and let the towel drop to the floor then, blow dried my hair until every curl was relaxed.

"How shall I wear you today? Up in a sophisticated style, or on my shoulders?" I said to my hair.

Troy had never seen my hair resting on my shoulders so; I decided to do the shoulders thing.

"All done" I sang. "And you look mar-va-lous" I smiled and kissed at myself.

I think I'll surprise Troy and wear my birthday suit for breakfast. That will shock the shingles off his rafters. I laughed to myself...this will be too funny seeing his expression.

I quickly opened the bathroom door, sashayed out and sang "Oh I'm so sorry!"

Troy was standing there in his bath robe, pants and shoes. And there was my stylist Sylvia, my manager Toni, and my personal assistant Alexis and, my SONS! Oh gosh, not my sons!

I couldn't grab for my towel because it was on the bathroom floor. No clothes anywhere. I only had a few changes of clothes with me for after the show to wear home. I felt my blood rise as my three sons looked at Troy..

Sylvia smiled, "Gurl, get yo grove on cos Sistah aint mad atcha."

Sylvia gave a brisk high five to Toni who was holding the most beautiful flowers in her hands. As I dipped back into the bathroom to retrieve the towel, Toni called out behind me.

"We were just about to leave. I just apologized to this, this hunk of a man and, told him we must have the wrong room. The hotel manager gave us a pass key to surprise you gurl."

The three ladies sang out, "SURPRISE!!!"

My youngest son grabbed the spread from the bed and hurried it over to me. My oldest son, Montel grabbed my middle son Dan almost out of midair.

"Here mom," my baby boy whispered. "Don't want you to catch a cold." I could have passed out.

"Baby I am so", I started.

"No worries mommy, dude is cool peoples. He told us he had slipped in to surprise you while you were in the shower." He winked.

"I brought you some flowers too. Great show last night." He kissed me on my cheek and gave me that look he usually does as if to say, "You earned it mommy, do you."

Soon my baby boy joined my oldest son in restraining Don and they left dragging him with them.

"Did you touch my moms' man? What did you do to my moms'? If you hurt my moms', I'll..." my sons were gone. And the three instigators took their place. They laid the flowers on the bed and quietly pulled the door closed behind them as they left blowing me kisses.

(To be continued by Troy)

When handed a bag of lemons, make lemonade. The last five minutes went by in a blur. Don't these folks know how to knock? I thought to myself.

Ren and I stood in our respective spots looking at our feet or, nondescript spots on the hotel room rug. At least I had the presence of mind to go to the bed and pull the comforter over our wet spot.

I don't think any explanation regarding my presence in the room so early in the morning, really fooled anyone. When Sylvia and Toni left, they had that, "*Gurl, you ain't fooling nobody and you betta have your story straight when we get together cause yo azz gon have to tell us every single thing including all the moans, groans, grunts and whatever pillow talk was going on while ya'll were turning each other out*", look on their faces.

There are times when words will not suffice and, this was one of them. While she was still burning a hole through the floor with her eyes, I closed the distance between us by taking her in my arms.

"I'm sorry darling," I said. "It happened so quickly, there was nothing I could do. I told them I had on the extra robe because I was going to help you with your hair. I hope you were not too embarrassed."

"Troy, I had all these things I wanted to say to you when I got out of the shower and almost blurted them out before I realized they were here. But, I won't let anything spoil what we shared." We took time to hold each other and, kiss deeply.

"Troy, we can't start this now, it's too close to check out time." Ren started.

"Check out? Oh I guess Toni didn't tell you when they went to the front desk they sent up a complimentary chit for another night on them? It seems like they enjoyed the perks that the concert provided. Patti mentioned the place during her closing comments and now all of their rooms are booked for every weekend this summer."

"Oh?" Ren responded. "I guess we need to find something to do."

"Well, I do have something in mind." I smiled.

"I bet you do." Ren replied. "Does it involve me tossing this sheet aside?" she asked referring to the spread wrapped around her.

"It certainly does." I answered. "But you do need to get dressed."

"Where are we going?" Lauren asked.

"Wear something dressy." I responded. "We're going to church and then to dinner at Mary Mac's".

I brought the rental unit around and we were soon on I-20 going east towards Augusta. We reached F.A.M.E. (First A.M.E.) Church just as they were starting the 11:30a.m., service.

Times like This

Reverend Bishop was sitting in the pulpit while the worship leader stirred things up. He smiled at me when he saw us sit down near the front.

When they asked for visitors to stand, I reluctantly stood because I knew that Ren would not stand if I hadn't. Reverend Bishop reminded the church as to who I was and asked about my daughter, their former Youth Pastor. After a thoroughly enjoyable worship experience, we left F.A.M.E. and headed towards downtown Atlanta.

Our reservation at Mary Mac was at 2p.m. We requested and received a table in the comer. It was secluded and somewhat romantic. The Tea Room was simple yet elegant. The aromas coming from the kitchen could have driven a hungry man crazy.

I ordered the strip and, Ren ordered the T-Bone. We also had some stir fry veggies, baked potatoes and, for drinks I ordered lemonade and Ren wanted water. In about 10 minutes, our meals were served while we munched on some delicious appetizers.

The server had looked at Ren and told her to save room for dessert while he winked. I was full; I could not have eaten another bite.

The Georgian Hotel was only 3 blocks away so we decided to walk. We walked along holding hands and chattering. When we reached the hotel, I gave the keys to a valet, told her where the car was parked and asked her to retrieve it and park it for me. Back in the room we got comfortable. I put on my robe again and Ren did the same.

"What would you like to do tonight?" I asked.

"You sure you want to know?" Lauren queried.

"Why not?" I responded.

"Well, I'd like to…

(To be continued by Lauren)

Troy was sitting on the edge of his seat, "What would you like to do?"

I ran my fingers through my hair, removing the bow that kept the pony tail at bay. My hair dropped about my shoulders. I could see by the way Troy's eyes lit up that he liked it. He smiled. "Well, what would you like to do?"

I began walking towards him, "I'd love to take a shower." I answered. Troy sat back in his seat. "What is it with you and showers?" he asked. I tilted my head ever so slightly to the side.

"Well, I thought you knew." I teased. Troy had a puzzled expression on his face.

"Thought I knew what?" he asked looking a little worried. I walked towards Troy crossing my feet like a cat, still teasing him.

"I don't know if I can tell you this or not." Troy sat straight up in the chair.

"You, you can tell me anything".

Troy swallowed hard. I reached him and curled up in his lap. I brushed my hair against his face. Troy took his hand and gently stroked my hair. Mmmmmm, I loved it. He asked softer now.

"What is it?" I leaned back so I could get a better look into his eyes. They were so big, so dark and so mysterious.

I answered softly, "I am really a..." I turned away trying not to laugh.

Troy shifted in the seat causing me to bounce a little in is lap. His arms almost instinctively grabbed my waist so as not to drop me.

"You're really what? What is it? Drugs? Alcohol what is it? You can tell me anything. I'm there for you."

I put my arms around his neck and placed my lips right at the tip of his ear as if afraid that someone else would hear my terrible secret.

Then I whispered, "I am really a mermaid and I want to take a shower with you."

I broke into almost hysterical laughter when I saw the expression of his face. Troy didn't know what to do. Who knew what horrors were racing through his mind. Then when he smiled, I knew I was in trouble. I jumped out of his lap and ran across the room.

"Come here you." Troy said softly.

I had never seen that expression on his face before.

"Come to me". Troy's eyes were so compelling. I felt my body moving towards his, didn't feel my feet moving though. I stopped just beyond his reach.

"Come to me now." Troy repeated even softer now.

Troy gently reached out to me and I seemingly drifted into his big black strong arms.

As Troy held me he whispered, "I'd love to take a shower with you my little mermaid." His eyes scanned my body and he laughed.

"Well, not little, but I'd still love to take a shower with you." I playfully slapped him.

Troy grabbed his face, "I'm just finding out all kinds of things about you today." he teased. "First I find out you're a dang fish and now I find out you're abusive. Third I find out that, I like it." Troy pulled me to himself and went right for the neck.

I just could not believe all this was happening. Never in my wildest of wildest dreams would I have ever thought I would meet someone like this. And, he was single, and he had a job. And he was so much fun and, intelligent to boot! I felt my clothing begin to fall to the floor.

"Troy" he never looked up or stopped.

"Yes my little starfish". His voice was muffled now as he began his journey downward.

"I'm thirsty. Can you get us some ice and bottled water? Please Troy?"

Troy continued, "We'll be in the shower soon, you won't be thirsty for long you little dolphin you." I shivered at his touch.

"I'm thirsty Troy." I repeated.

Troy smiled and sang, "I'll be right back."

As he vanished through the door almost running, I quickly grabbed my bag. I had a pair of thongs that I never wore. They were red hot and black lace. I slipped them into the comer chair. After the shower I would slip into them.

I grabbed the matching bra that had no cups in it. Fredericks of Hollywood indeed, I smiled to myself. I removed the rest of my clothing to get ready for the shower. No, I didn't really want water, not then anyway.

I could see that in Troy's haste to get some bottled water he didn't shut the door. I started towards the door in my birthday suit. I looked down at my body and noticed how toned it was becoming. Being with Troy was doing me some good. I don't think crunches could accomplish what I was looking at and, they weren't as fun either.

I chuckled to myself and reached for the door. It flew open and in darted Ricki!

"Ooooo chile" he sang, "It's too early to be naked! Honey Chile, I gots ta show you sumthin."

I was shocked. "Ricki, what the....?"

Troy rushed into the room behind him dropping the ice and the bottled water and, snatched Ricki by the collar.

"Troy wait!" I shouted. Ricki wiggled free,

"Hold it big fella. I want the same thing she wants"! I grabbed for the covers but they were so tight on the bed.

"Relax gurlfriend" Ricki sang. "Your secret is safah.....with me-ah".

I jumped under the sheets, they were crisp and clean and my favorite color for sheets, black.

"Who is this clown?" Troy asked grabbing him again by the shirt.

"Oh hurt me, hurt me good." Ricki sang. Troy swung Ricki around.

"Negro I will stomp a mud hole in you're as...."

"Baby wait!" I protested. "This is Ricki our designer. Please don't hurt him."

Ricki reached up, "Please...what she said...I'm family." Troy threw Ricki on the floor.

"I don't believe this. Have you people EVER heard of knocking?" Ricki slid slowly across the floor away from the raging hurricane Troy.

"The- the- the door was open. I-I didn't know..I mean, we never knock. Lauren is always alone." Ricki turned to me, "Sorry Precious."

Troy removed his robe and gave it to me. Looking at Ricki, he shouted, "Get up fool!"

Ricki scrambled to his feet. "I, I....sorry Lauren. I didn't know you would be in here with the incredible hunk...I mean hulk." His eyes quickly darted over Troy's body. "I only came to show you the afternoon reviews. You killed it last night gurlfriend." Troy walked to the door.

"And you've got half a second to get out of here before I kill you." Ricki scurried to the door. "And tell your people to start knocking...Lauren's not alone anymore."

As Ricki reached the door, Troy grabbed his shoulder and said calmly, "You alright sweetness?" Ricki quickly nodded.

"Good, no harm, no fowl bro. Just knock for Pete sakes, ok dude?" Ricki nodded again and was out the door.

Troy locked the door and checked it twice. He then placed the privacy lock on and double checked it. Troy turned to me and placed his hands on his hips. He stood silent for a second then pointed at me.

"You must have been a Playboy bunny in another life," Troy smiled. "You sure have a way of letting people see you naked."

I sank under the covers and pulled the robe around me. Ricki had a bigger mouth than any woman in the Industry. I knew I was going to catch it now from the gang. I felt almost depressed.

Troy sat on the bed, "Would you like me to get you some more ice?"

I grabbed his wrist. "Please, don't you dare go out that door again until I get dressed!" Troy laughed and cupped my face in his hand.

"You look wonderful. And they all know you do. I mean look at you. You have the body of a woman in her twenties."

I pulled the covers closer to me. Now I was really depressed. Tomorrow I had to get back to work. It would be business as usual. I turned my head so he wouldn't see the tears that were trying to well up in my eyes. I felt Troy's hand stroking my hair again. Man, I loved it when he did that.

Troy continued talking but I wasn't listening. I couldn't listen. In just a few hours all of this would be over. Troy leaned closer to me and I quickly grabbed his neck putting my chin on his shoulder so he wouldn't see my expression. The robe had opened so it was my bare chest on his.

"Oh Troy, I am so glad that I met you.....and at the same time, would it have been better for me if I had not? Ricki was so right and I never realized it until now, I HAVE always been alone. And they always just came into my room so openly because there had never been a reason to knock. We were all just girls like that...and Ricki too. And, we never knocked".

I felt Troy lifting me from the bed. My towel dropped to the floor as he headed towards the shower.

"You sure you don't want some of that nice cold ice now?" He asked as he reached the shower.

I shook my head and quietly answered, "All I want now is something black and hot."

At my words his grip tightened. Troy lowered me slowly to the floor. I turned and started the shower.....
(To be continued by Troy)

Lauren felt me lifting her from the bed. Her towel dropped to the floor as I headed towards the shower.

"You sure you don't want some of that nice cold ice now?" I asked as we reached the shower.

Lauren shook her head and quietly answered, "All I want now is something black and hot."

At those words my grip tightened as well as my shaft. I lowered Ren slowly to the floor. She turned and started the shower as I stood there stripping my clothes off. Bending over like Ren was, left her round apple bottom perched up for me.

I walked up behind Lauen and began to gently caress her buns. Lauen began to purr like a sex kitten and rotated her butt in a very suggestive and seductive way. I simply could not resist and planted a kiss on those buns. All I needed was some butter to go on those hot, tasty buns. When my lips touched her cheeks, she pushed back to make sure she was giving me all that I desired.

The bathroom began to steam from the hot water so we decided to get into the shower. Lauren had a complete assortment of body washes, gels, and they all seemed to be from either body works or Victoria's Secret. There was lavender, apple cinnamon, jasmine and others. Lauren picked a bottle, opened it and gave it to me. Then she selected a loofah from her basket and gave that to me also.

"Cleanse me", she ordered. I went over her entire body and the foamy suds completely covered her. Then I stood back, admiring her body and my handy work.

"You're not done yet Mister. You missed a few spots." Lauren said.

"Where"? I asked.

"Here" Ren said pointing to her golden triangle.

"I think I can fix that," I smiled as I applied gel to the satiny pubic hair.

While soaping her body, I took the opportunity to let my hands explore. I closed my eyes as if I were blind and let my hands do the seeing for me.

I started with the lower legs, moved behind the knees and then the thighs. By the time I got to the inner thighs, my hands were seeing perfect symmetry.

Lauren opened her legs slightly as my fingers touched the center of her womanhood. With the foamy suds all over my fingers as well as all over her, my fingers slid into some otherwise tight places and lingered for a little while.

"That wasn't the spot I was saying that you missed", Ren smiled, "But you are doing a good job....don't stop."

As I began moving slowly in and out between her legs, Ren's breathing quickened and the nipples on her full breasts showed their excitement. They gave the sistah away. I continued fingering her until I knew she wanted to cum. Then I eased off and, continued kissing my sweet baby.

More Love

"You're falling down on the job." I teased. "I only have soap on my hands. What do you intend to do about that?" Without saying a word, Lauren body rubbed me.

"Turn around," she said, "so I can get your back". I turned my back to her and she rubbed me again. Lauren then took a loofah and began a hand job.

With soapy slippery hands, Lauren started stroking me with up, down and twisting motions. Then she peeled back my foreskin and, focused on my swollen purple head.

Ren had me backed against the shower wall and, was making me want to move. When Ren knew I could go no further, she intensified her stroking while looking directly into my eyes.

As she stroked, the hot water cascaded off her breasts and somehow my arousal factor grew. By now, Lauren knew how I sounded when I was about to cum, so she gave my shaft a tight squeeze and my orgasm subsided.

"Let's finish this shower baby. I have a surprise for you." I said.

"What is it?" Ren wanted to know.

"If I told you, it would not be a surprise any longer would it?"

We finished and got out of the shower and I tossed Ren her robe then, I put mine on and, we headed for the pool on the top floor. Once we got there, instead of going to the pool, we went to the hot tub. I had reserved it for two hours, just for us.

Ren squealed in delight and walked to the hot tub in front of me. The swish, swish action of her butt in front of me brought back the hard on that I had lost when we got onto the elevator.

Apparently Ren felt she needed to continue her cleaning so she grasped my shaft and began stroking again. Using the bouncing of water, Lauren put her legs around me and presented her honey pot to my lower 40. As I entered her, she shuddered and...

(To be continued by Lauren)

MY LOVE IS A MOUNTAIN

My love is a mountain
oh so very tall
you can barely see it's peak.
There are clouds up there
in the air up there.
Sometimes it can get dark. ..
ON YOUR MARK!

My mountain has sharp edges
you can get hurt if you fall.
There's danger if you let down your guard.
But the beauty you see
lives inside of me
it hasn't been conquered yet .....
GET SET!

My mountain has soft curves and deep crevices.
Exploration is well worth the time.
Plant your feet and be sure .
Hold on tight and endure .
If you know that you know .
GO!

My love is a mountain of wonders to see.
If you're up for the task. ..
CLIMB ME!
© Psoemetry 2007

I closed my eyes as I felt his massive flesh entering me. Then a thought crossed my mind.

"Troy....did you lock the door?"

The hot soothing water was swirling aggressively around us now. Troy held me tightly as if he were trying to save his life....and mine.

"Y-yes" he answered quickly. Remembering his track record of us and doors I asked again.

"Troy, are you sure?" His lips were deep into my neck now.

"I did, I promise you I did." he answered.

Feeling a little panicky I insisted, "Troy, can you please check?" Troy only held me tighter. "Troy!"

Troy ignored me, lifted me gently and, suddenly I could feel water rushing all around me. What was he doing? He's about to take me under water...I can't believe....

"Troy wait!"

I took as large a breath of air as my lungs could hold and, we were under. I could feel our bodies spinning as if caught in a whirl wind. Water was churning from all sides of me and, I held on for dear life as Troy moved deep inside of me.

I was terrified yet the sensation was unbelievable. There was all kind of movement. We were intertwined like wild tangled roots growing free.

Troy lunged upwards. I could see the water surface as we rushed towards it. I held on and tightened my legs around his waist grasping his neck tighter as this man stood straight up. I gasped for air, once, twice and we were going back down.

I almost screamed as the water crashed around us and, then....bubbles. I don't know if I was able to hang on because of fear or, if it just felt too good to let go. The entire scene was just crazy.

More swirling, more bubbles. I could feel my breasts gently being nibbled on, then more aggressively. My mind was exploding with thoughts. I no longer cared about the door being locked or even closed. I felt, wild and dirty and clean and OH MY GOSH!

Troy was going up again! We surfaced. His muscles ripped under my grasp. All of them at once and at the same time individually. It was just too crazy! I shook the water out of my eyes and grasped for air. Troy was in total control.

I looked into his eyes and I grabbed all the air that I possibly could just in case he submerged again. The expression on Troy's face was so intense.

His body began to vibrate fiercely. I felt my thighs tighten around him. Almost convulsing, Troy dove again. Ohhhhhhhh SPLASH!!! Did I get enough air ths time? My mind was spinning. We were on the floor of the hot tub and Troy was riding me like a mad man. And I loved it! He battled against the force of the water rushing everywhere.

"Oh god, I'm going to die." I thought as the last of my air started leaving my lungs.

There was nothing I could do. I relaxed my legs around this beast and almost instinctively he darted for the surface again. Troy gently placed me on the step of the hot tub. I gasped for air and he dove. My chest was heaving now as the water dripped off of me.

(To be continued by Troy)

"STAIRS"

While ascending the stairs,
I looked to behold your beauty.
Beautiful brown legs perfectly formed.
Thighs that can only be called friendly.
I held my breath as you began to ascend.
The hem of your dress pulled to your thighs
taking slow steps to tease the heart.
Knowing that I am watching.
You glanced over your shoulder
and smiled a smile of tender care.

Paused, so I could take you in
with eyes that penetrated all.
The sensuous silk covered little
exposed round buns
showed the separation one from the other
and the space where they parted.
You turned around and faced me.
Upon the deck you sat.
Legs teasingly open and starring at me.
My eyes transfixed to an intimate site.

The inner thighs were smooth and soft.
Stray pubes spry and black.
The silk so thin, barely a barrier;
So inviting.
You toweled your leg
while the other stood open.
I drew closer as I ascended
fully aroused by your intimate aura.
Handing me the towel you asked
to help remove the sand.

I could have reached out to touch your essence.

The dampness that had begun to show.
Our eyes met, our hearts had too.
We began to kiss again.
My hands found familiar places,
I felt yours in theirs.
Your sensuous stroking stirred my loins,
Made the rhythm of my body sway.
Made the hair on my head cry out of love
Made my body respond to you.

©The Ebony Poet

She relaxed her legs around me and almost instinctively I darted for the surface again then, I gently placed Ren on the stairs leading from the hot tub.

As she stood there on the stairs, Ren closed her eyes and her breathing began to return to normal. Her luscious breasts were heaving and, they made a delicious sight.

As I stood admiring her assets and my engine was beginning to whine again. We took another shower together, donned our robes and went back to the room to get dressed.

But instead of our regular clothes, I had something special delivered for both of us. Black leather pants, boots, black leather vests and caps...dress appropriate for riding my motorcycle.

The Harley was in the valet parking area but, I didn't trust the valet to retrieve it so I went and got it myself. I roared up to the entry of the hotel and told Ren to hop on.

Her leather pants were tight and her bottom was beautifully encased in stretch leather. As Ren rode behind me, the vibration of the motorcycle caused a vibration in her pussy and I felt it behind me. I was going pretty fast and, she held on for dear life.

We took I-85 past the airport and found my secluded little cabin off the highway. Once we got into the cabin, my hands were all over that leather. I sucked her breasts while her hands stroked my engorged staff. When I came, it was intense and, Ren had a hand full of cum. As she lie her on her back with a pillow under her butt, Lauren presented her cherry in great fashion.

I started by sucking her toes and worked my way up to her inner thighs. As I licked and sucked that succulent meat, she began a soft moan. I nibbled and kissed, as my face brushed her pubic hair and I could feel the dampness.

My tongue traced the outline of her pussy lips and then back to her clit. It was hidden behind the hood and I wanted to coax it out. After a few licks, it came to life and had a head of its own. I sucked it into my mouth and I could feel Lauren inhale a large gulp of air. Then I slid my tongue inside of Ren and began to lick her smooth pussy walls.

With my hands cupping her buns I ate her. I licked, kissed, lapped and enjoyed her core. Lauren's thighs were wrapped around my neck and each time I hit a sensitive spot, she squeezed me harder. We were in rhythm.

My tongue matched the tempo of her thrusts back towards me. Her orgasm was rough. She bucked, twisted, turned and, squeezed my neck. At one point I thought Lauren would surely break it but, I was not going to stop and cheat her out of a great experience.

When Lauren came, a torrent of liquid squirted from deep inside her and wet my face. We lay there, our bodies quivering, shaking, and feeling quite satiated.

(To be continued by Lauren)

"Troy, we'd better get back" I touched him on his shoulder then, went to the bathroom and quickly washed. Suddenly, my phone began ringing.

Hello?" It was Toni. "Hi Toni. What's going on?"

Toni was all excited. She said she hadn't called me because she knew I was probably with my new man. I ran my fingers through my hair as Troy got up and came over to me. He kissed me on the back of my neck.

"I'm going to wash up real quick and we can go."

Troy gave me a loving tap on the bottom and then, disappeared into the bathroom. How well I knew that this week would soon come to an end. Troy was singing. I could hear the water running.

"Wow" I thought. "I'm sorry Toni...what? Alright, alright I'll be there. Just give me about two hours. Wait! I'm not at the hotel; I'll need about two hours. Alright then, bye....bye Toni!"

I closed my phone up as Troy came back into the room. He looked so good in his leather. The smell of leather....I loved it.

"Are you hungry?" Troy asked. I shook my head. "What's the matter babe?" I gathered my few things.

"I've got a meeting tonight."

Troy kissed me. "And after the meeting?"

I shook my head again. "It's going to be a long night for me Troy". He smiled and grabbed his helmet.

"No worries. We'll still hook up after." Troy handed me my helmet and looked into my eyes. I could feel the tears coming again.

"What's the matter?" I placed the helmet over my head. "Can we just go Troy?" He sat down.

"Yes, as soon as you tell me what the matter is."

I headed for the door and pulled it open quickly, "Let's just please go."

Troy was right behind me now. He gently reached over me and shut the door. Were we fighting? It didn't feel like a fight, at least none that I was accustomed to.

Troy took me by my hand and led me back to the bed. He sat down first pulling me onto his lap. I turned away but he tenderly brought my face back to meet his.

Brushing my hair out of my eyes Troy again asked. "What's the matter?"

I sighed very deeply, "it's over" Troy sat back and looked surprised.

"You're breaking up with me?" he asked. "Oh wait, you can't break up with me because I never asked you to be my woman."

I looked at Troy, and standing, headed back to the door. He playfully ran and shut the door again.

"Can I ask you first before you dump me?"

I was irritated, "Ask me what Troy? Ask me what?"

Troy smiled, "If you'll be my woman."

I turned and looked at the door then at Troy. "Troy, I would love to be your woman, but I can't do the long distance relationship thing. I just can't. You live in Texas and I live in Atlanta. My work is here or where ever the gig might be and you..."

Troy took my hand, "My work is where ever I tell it to be.
I'm not tied down by corporate America. I'm a writer so where ever I lay my hat is where I say it is, so, yes or no?" I looked at my watch.

"I'm...! I just don't know. I mean these few days together were just wonderful but...I mean it was magic but once the magic ends then what?" Troy pulled me to his chest and embraced me.

"I mean what we just experienced isn't ever day normal. It was exciting but it was.....it was." Troy pushed me back from him so he could see my face.

"It was what? And how do you know it was...it was...you know?" I pulled away from him.

"We have to go. I can't be late." Troy stepped in front of the door.

"We need to talk about this Lauren. We need to talk about this now." I stood there silently. "What are you afraid of? Do you want me to say I'll never ever leave you? Do you want me to say I'll always love you? Do you want me to say that I'll make crazy love to you every day several times a day? What do you want me to say? Do you want me to ask you to marry me? What do you want from me Lauren? If you don't tell me I won't know. I mean nothing is broken here...what's the problem?"

I spun around, "My heart is breaking okay? My heart is breaking because what we had this weekend was magical and I don't want to lose it. I don't want to watch you walk or ride or fly or however the heck you're going to leave my life. I've been alone for a long time; a very long time. And, then you come and take that loneliness away."

"And now, tomorrow will be business as usual. I'll go back to my home and my work and you'll go back to Texas. I don't want a computerized lover. I need you here with me so I can hold you, touch you, smell you."

The tears were falling now, like rivers. Troy opened the door.

"I'll be at the hotel during your meeting baby doll." Troy said as he reached for my hand.

"We need to talk. You don't have any reason to be afraid of losing me. Let me get you to your meeting then after we'll get something to eat and then we'll talk. After what we've shared there is no way I'm giving you up without a fight".

"Every part of my body from my mind, my eyes, my heart and parts south are deeply in love with you. Can we talk later?"

I nodded my head yes, and soon we were on his bike again and flying.

(To be continued by Troy)

Stunned beyond belief, I followed Ren out of the cabin door and out to where the bike was parked. Lauren had a distant look in her eyes and was looking out over the lake.

I started to walk toward her, but she turned and looked at me. I could see the resolve in her eyes. I slipped my helmet on my head and started the bike. Ren climbed on behind me and we started the trip back to Atlanta. It had only taken us 35 minutes to get there, but it seemed like it was taking hours to get back.

I was glad that I was riding in front as tears welled in my eyes. It had been years since I had trusted anyone with my heart. And Lauren had broken it to pieces.

Five years ago, I had given my heart to Mira. We planned a June wedding date. Mira called me every day to tell me what she was doing and to bounce ideas off me. Her budget had been unlimited as I had opened a checking account for her with a gold card at Barbados National Bank. Mira told me about the banquet director and how helpful he had been in helping her make arrangements.

They would go to dinner in the hotel and Mira would share with him all that she had done that day and what she needed, He would give her directions and make calls to make it easy for her.

Then the daily calls stopped coming. Mira would call every two to three days explaining how busy she had been. I knew she was busy so I had no problem with it. I knew my baby was working very, very hard. I asked Mira if she needed anything else and she said "no", she was satisfied.

The anniversary of our engagement was that next weekend so I decided to fly there and surprise her. Plus, I was damn horny by now and, I needed some tender loving that only Mira was going to provide me.

I called the office and had my secretary get the pilot on the phone to get the corporate jet ready for the trip. The plane landed in Barbados and I had a limo take me to the hotel.

I had picked up a diamond tennis bracelet for a gift for Mira and I knew she would be so surprised after working day and night to plan a grand wedding. I went to the front desk, got a room keycard and took the elevator up to the penthouse suite.

I opened the door and went inside. All of the lights were off but music was playing. I had one light bag and I dropped that on the thick carpeted floor and, headed for the bedroom. I was going to surprise her, so I stripped out of my clothes so Mira would wake up next to a naked man in her bed.

I heard the noises first and I knew what it was as soon as I heard it. I thought perhaps Mira had been horny too and had ordered an adult movie.

I opened the door and slowly entered the room. Mira's back was to me. She was on her knees straddling a man and riding him. She was pumping for all she was worth. I stood there looking at them in stark disbelief.

He was the first to see me and yelled..."Who the fuck are you man?!"

Mira screamed, "Oh no," grabbed a sheet and turned to look at me.

Heartbroken I spoke, "Happy engagement anniversary Mira" I tossed the tennis bracelet to her.

"It's not what it looks like" she cried. I never looked back.

I went downstairs, had the front desk call the limo and I headed for the airport. By the time I got to the plane, it had been fueled and was ready for takeoff. I never saw Mira again after those brief minutes in the bedroom.

I called my secretary from the plane and had her close the accounts and cancel the gold cards then, I buried myself in my work and swore off dating. I would NOT go through that heartbreak ever again...

Ren and I arrived at the hotel on my bike and I drove it to the front entrance. I asked the valet to keep my bike while I walked Ren to the elevator. Lauren pushed the button to take her to her room. She had to change because she had appointments.

I smiled at Lauren and told her to take care, that I would see her later. I gave her a gentle kiss on the lips and the elevator doors closed tight.

I went back outside, got on my bike and headed back to my summer house in Stone Mountain. Once there, I put the bike away, grabbed my bags, told the housekeeper I was heading back to Austin and, ask her to take care of everything.

At the airport I was escorted directly to my corporate jet when I got to Hartsfield. As soon as I got on board the pilot was given clearance to taxi to the runway.

Once the sleek jet climbed and banked to the west and picked up speed the fluffy clouds rolled by and we cut through them. I put some music on and picked up something to read. Just as a coincidence, Anita Baker was playing. I closed the book, closed my eyes and the jet streaked towards Austin and healing....

(To be completed by Ren)

Endings?

I couldn't wait to get back to Troy. The idea of his not being in my life was almost unbearable. What must Troy be thinking right now? My heart ached terribly as if at any moment it would explode.

I was running late for my meeting. I hurried to my room, showered quickly, then dressed for the meeting. I was so late by now. As quickly as I could I rushed to the meeting. When I entered the conference room, everyone was already seated and waiting for me.

"Where have you been, we've been waiting for you" Toni whispered as she showed me to my seat. The others glanced at their watches and looked nervously in my direction.

I noticed two very distinctly dressed gentlemen seated at the table also checking the time. "I apologize for being late" I began. "Something came up and…." Toni patted my hand. "It's fine dear, we're all here now." She began speaking. "The reason we are here tonight is to go over the recent show. I want to let everyone know right now that the reviews were very very good. In fact, they were much better than good. They were awesome!"

The room broke into applause as she continued," Ricki will go over the stats" Ricki stood and began speaking as my thoughts drifted away until I could no longer hear a word he was saying. The only thing I could think of was returning to my room to resolve any issues that had come up in our relationship now.

The only thing I could think of or wanted to do was to get back there to Troy. The idea of Troy not being in my life was almost unbearable. What must he be thinking right now? My heart ached terribly as if at any moment it would explode.

All of a sudden everyone was hugging and dancing. Toni introduced me to Walter and James our new investors. Walter was very tall and very dark with an athletic build. He extended his hand and I accepted it.

"You're quite an artist." he smiled.

Ricki slapped me on my back, "Oh don't be shy. Give him a hug. We hug around here!"

I cut my eyes at him as Walter opened his arms to embrace me; his new investment. What Ricki was actually hoping was that this would be his opening to get a hug himself from this man. I quickly hugged Walter and thanked him for his interests in our projects.

Then James stepped up. He was dressed to the tee and smelled like money. As James extended his arms for his hug, Ricki eagerly awaited his turn. The diamonds on this man's watch almost blinded me. I embraced James as well.

"Thank you James, we appreciate you both. This was, rather is indeed good news." I smiled and gathered my things.

"Hold up, where you goin?" Sylvia asked. I looked at my watch.

"I have a meeting with Troy." Sylvia grabbed my arm.

"You talkin 'bout Mr. Ever Ready?" She laughed. Gurrrrl, hunk of a man? Y'all just can't keep your hands off each other can you chile? I hear ya tho." She popped her gum and patted her stylish do.

"If he was in my bed 24/7 three days straight and the only reason I would get OUT of bed was to shower and start all over again.....huntee gurl uh uh !!. I'd be rushing back too ya heard? But listen here Sistah...this here is bizznis ya hearing me? What would it look like you skippin out now? We 'bout ta go to a party in yo honor. In yo" she pranced and pointed to me, "Yo honor. You got ta holla at Rocky lata."
I looked at her. 'Oh, no she didn't!'

"Listen Sylvia...." I started.

"Naw naw naw sistah gurl, you comin with us here."

She motioned to everyone in the room.

"But I have to..."

Walter touched my arm. "You can ride with me in my limo, Super Star" he smiled. "Toni and Alexi will also be riding with me. Then we can discuss your upcoming tour that starts in one week. You, my dear, are about to really blow up." He motioned an explosion and everyone laughed.

Walter gently took my arm to escort me out of the room, the lights were turned off and, the door was shut after the last person exited.

When we arrived at the celebration, it was just amazing. No corners were cut and you could clearly see that someone was very, very pleased with the product we had to offer. There was food everywhere. The aroma was so inviting. I walked from table to table looking.

"What are you waiting for? Dig in!" A strange voice came from behind me. When I turned, some back in the day pimp daddy looking guy stood smiling. His gold teeth flashed at me as he smiled.

"My name is Roger Willgo from Willgo Enterprises." He extended his hand. I shook it. As he began loading his plate he kept talking.

"You see my slogan is...if you want somebody to go.....Roger... Will Go"! He started laughing almost uncontrollably.

"Oh Father, please help me." I thought.

"Try some of the bourbon chicken. It's really good. I had five helpings already. I mean it is goooood!" He pushed me with his elbow and continued loading his plate.

Seemingly impatient for me to lift my plate and begin preparing it, he took a plate and fixed it and handed it to me.

"Don't worry about watching your figure baby gurl" he winked. "I can do that fo ya." Roger must have thought he was hilarious the way he was laughing.

I smiled and took the plate. Leaning towards him I said, "And if I need you to go?"

He perked up and almost sang. "Roger Will ...go" Roger burst into laughter again. Then I smiled at him.

"Get it?" His laughter stopped.

"Oh, you...want me to ...go?" I kept smiling sweetly.

"Will you please? I don't mean any harm. I just, you know..."

He bowed his head, "No prob baby gurl. I'll be just a hoot and a holla away if you need me." I thanked Roger for fixing my plate and began walking towards Alexis. Ricki intercepted me.

"This is Sho Gun, he's a famous rapper. Isn't he delicious?" I looked at Ricki.

"Here, have some chicken." I answered.

"Ooooo!" he squealed. "I love bourbon chicken. However did you know?" I continued walking.

"Alexis, I need to go." I took her arm. Alexis was sipping a glass of champagne.

"Go? Go where; to the little girls room? OK I'll go with you." I shook my head.

"No chile. I need to go back to my hotel room." She pulled her arm away from me.

"Chile, are you crazy; or nuts?" She folded her arms. "Do you see all these fine and rich men up in here at this party? I got champagne in my glass. Did you hear me? CHAMPAGNE!!! You already got your naked hunk back in the bed just waiting on you to come bouncing through the door, I gots ta get me one."

"Alexis, I am not playing. I need to go." I protested.

Alexis took another sip of her glass and smiled at a young man who passed by us. He smiled his interest back at her and continued walking. He turned a few times to look back at us as he continued to walk. Each time his smile grew larger as we watched him.

Alexis shook her head and lifted her glass. "Now ya see, THAT'S what I'm talkin 'bout." I took her glass.

"I need to go now Alexis." Alexis took her glass back and motioned for a refill.

"What you want me to do Ren, huh? What do you want me to do?" Her glass was promptly refilled.

"Thank you baby," she smiled to the waiter. "Listen Ren, I didn't drive. I rode with you in the limo. What is up with you? Did he hit that so good you can't be away from him for even a second? This is your big day. We all just got paid and you're actin like the reviews were terrible and you bout ta get shut down."

"You just don't understand." I objected. Another waiter passed us and offered me a glass. "No thanks hon", I said softly then, continued.

"You just don't understand...." Alexis held her hand up to the waiter.

"I'll have another." I couldn't believe it. Alexis was drinking like a fish.

"What are you doing Alexis?" She smiled and began to giggle.

"Gurrrrl, I"m bout to get tore up." Alexis started laughing. "Then one of these fiiiiine brothas up in here is gonna take me home and take advantage of me."

"Have you lost your dag gone mind? What the heck is wrong with you? I mean come on Alexis! Are you serious?" Alexis took the glass to the head.

"I ain't had a good lay in weeks. Make that months. I'm itching for a reeeeal good scratchin." The same young man passed again. This time he stopped.

"Hi ladies. What's good? I'm Teddy." Alexis squealed and took his extended elbow and cooed.

"Oh my Teddy Bear," She winked and they left.

"Alexis!" I called after her. But she wasn't hearing me.

I saw James in the comer speaking with Toni. I hurried over to them both.

"Excuse me." I began. James turned.

"Oh, hi Superstar, we were just talking about you." I lifted my hand.

"I'm sorry. I just needed to mention that Alexis is getting drunk and some guy named Teddy just took her off somewhere." James looked over my shoulder and motioned for one of the security officers to come over.

"Look man, go find Teddy. He's with one of the new family. Tell him to keep it chilly." The giant nodded and hurried off.

"Now," James continued. "With that taken care of, let's talk shop. Everyone should be ready. Come with us into the conference room. We need to go over some things and get some papers signed."

It was looking like it would truly be an all nighter. I hoped that Troy would make himself comfortable in my room or even his. Maybe I should call him and let him know that things were running really late.

His phone began ringing, but he didn't pick up. He must be really upset with me. Ya think? Everything I ever wanted was right through that door; contracts, money, blingage, the whole nine.

"Well gurl." I thought to myself. "Gone and git cho money."

When I was finally dropped off, it was well after 4 a.m. I rushed up to my room half expecting Troy to be asleep in my bed. Oh how I wanted to just hold him one more time before he left for Texas. Just once more, if he would let me. Maybe he would kiss me and gently tell me my fears were for nothing and that he would never leave me. Not ever.

I scanned my key in the door and noticed that the room was empty. I turned on the lights and went through the suite. No one was there. He must have decided to stay in his room.

I threw my body across my bed and tried to sleep but, sleep wouldn't come. I'll see him at check out. I decided to pack and get ready to leave. It was a long few hours.

I decided to wait until about 9am and go to his room. Maybe he'll have breakfast with me once more before he left. No one answered at his room. I went to the front desk. Maybe he went out to have breakfast. Maybe the front desk knew where he was.

"Good morning. I'm trying to find Mr. Johnson." The clerk looked up. His eyes lit up.

"It's you! I saw you. You opened for Patti Labelle. I love spoken word. I bought your CD." He reached under the desk. "I knew you were staying here. Can I get your autograph? Can you put to Wilson; to Wilson Gregory, with love. My biggest fan." I touched his hand and smiled.

"How about if I put, 'thanks Wilson from Lauren' and date it." He smiled and rocked from side to side.

"That'll work." He was rubbing his hands together.

I was so moved. No one had ever reacted like that to me before. I guess things were changing for real. He read over the signature as if it were pure gold.

"Oh and Mr. Johnson checked out yesterday. He autographed a copy of his book for me. I got that yesterday."

My heart dropped to the floor and broke. No it didn't break, it disintegrated.

"He left yesterday?" I repeated in disbelief. The young man was still admiring my autograph.

"Yes ma'am he left." I shook my head.

"Well, did he say anything?" Now Wilson was holding a camera. He called for one of the other clerks.

"Oh he just said he was finished here," was Wilson's answer. "Can I take a picture with you please?" I forced a smile.

"Sure baby." I softly answered. "Come on and get your picture."

One picture turned into 27 as others joined in on the photo shoot and continued until the camera film was all used up. I returned to my room, gathered my things then, checked out.

I thank God that I was kept so busy over the next few weeks. The nights were the hardest for me. Troy wouldn't answer my calls so I finally gave up and, threw myself deeper into my work.

My poetry became sharper, more alive and filled with emotion. I began getting calls to do guest spots on shows like Oprah and Ellen.

Once I hit Oprah there was no stopping me. All she had to say is, "This artist is going places" and the CD sales shot to platinum. Platinum for spoken word, Oh my goodness!

Life was really good, for everybody. New cars were rolling in, new homes, and new lovers. Hurrmph! This should have been the time Troy and I could truly be spending enjoying each other. But then, my time was so limited, it's possible the end results would have still been the same.

My tour dates increased over the next few years. I was all over the papers and, selling CD's and books of poetry. I had even written a book about my life experiences in a book titled, 'The Concert'. In no time at all, it made the best sellers list. I had everything I could have possibly ever wanted. And, I kept up with the papers as well, enough to know what was going on in Troy's life also.

Troy had written four books since the last time I saw him and, they were all best sellers. Troy was always in the news for literary awards and the like. He did a lot of community service as well.

I remember once, my son came back from the grocery store with an Ebony Magazine. Troy was on the cover smiling and looking as handsome as ever with a woman at his side, who was also smiling.

I felt my heart breaking all over again. In a way, that was kind of good because I thought my heaert was gone. I spent hours trying to imagine what could have possibly gone wrong. Was it something I said or did?

We were supposed to talk after my meeting. Troy said 'ok', and then he left. Was he using me? Oh my gosh, Troy was using me! The tears flowed, again.

I recall a day Ricki came over. Ricki was even blinging now. He said he had become concerned about my weight loss. Ricki stopped by a popular chicken joint and picked up my favorite dish. Honey BBQ wings, on the bone, with two strawberry deserts on the side.

We sat relaxing in my home. He was many things, this Little Ricki as I sometimes affectionately called him. But when it came to real friendship, Ricki was there for me always.

On this particular day, he bounced in the chair as we ate, and instructed me to relive that last night Troy and I had together.

"Don't forget the juicy stuff honey." he sang snacking on a wing.

Naturally I skipped the juicy stuff, (he was so silly, bless his darling heart.) After I finished sharing my tearful story, my the tears were gushing. Ricki handed me a tissue and popped me in the head with his fingertips.

"You silly goose." he sang. "You told Troy to leave you and he did."

Through drenched eyes I asked, "What are you talking about Ricki? I loved Troy, why would I tell him to leave me? I was afraid he would leave me, and he did."

I leaned on the arm of the sofa and just sobbed. Ricki pushed his chicken aside and sat beside me. He pulled me to him so that I was now crying on his shoulders.

"There, there now," he comforted. He handed me a ton more tissues . "Look at you, a big star like you." I dried my eyes to no avail.

"Why Ricki? Why did Troy leave me like that? No good-bye, no nothing. And Troy never returned my calls." Ricki took me by my shoulders and looked me square in my eyes.

I could always depend on Ricki to be straight with me. Ah well, at least be honest with me.

"Duh," he sang. "Hence the words...."IT'S OVER!!!" Ricki repeated. I looked through the drenched tissues.

"What?"

Ricki repeated, "It's over! You silly, you told Troy it was over." I sat up in disbelief.

"I never said that!" Ricki nodded his head.

"Yes you did, you just told me you did." I was standing now.

"I was talking about what we shared for that long weekend was over. I didn't know how to deal with Troy having to go back to Texas. I didn't mean I wanted to end the relationship. I was afraid it would end by Troy going back to Texas. Oh god no"! Ricki stood and touched my shoulders.

"Honey," Ricki spoke softer now. "You think being a writer you could have expressed yourself a little bit better on that one." Pulling away I ran my fingers through my hair and picked up the phone.

"I never meant that Ricki." I put the phone back down.

"When Troy asked you to be his woman, did you answer?" Ricki asked. I picked up the phone again and held it to my ear.

Ricki repeated, "Well did you answer?" I asked placing the phone back down, "Answer what?"

Ricki scurried over to where I stood and removed the phone from my hands and hung it up.

"Did you answer the man's question?" I lifted the phone again.

"What question Ricki? What question?" Ricki took the phone again. This time he kept it.

"You're not even listening to me now." Ricki walked off with the phone. I raised my voice.

"Ricardo, I am upset now in case you didn't notice!" Ricki tossed the phone.

"I told you never to call me that! I know you're upset Ice Cream, but that's the problem with you."

I hated when Ricki called me Ice Cream. I could feel my temperature rising now.

"Ricardo, what are you talking about?" Ricki was flailing his arms now.

"That's so like you Ice Cream. When you get upset you NEVER listen. You never ever listen!" We could tell you the room is on fire and it's all about you. You never hear us when you're upset, and you didn't hear Troy either!" I was shocked.

"What?" Ricki's face was a deep red now as he dropped himself into a chair and folded his arms.

"There I said it" he replied.

I walked slowly over to him asking, "I never listen?"

Ricki bounced in his chair and repeated, "Never."

I knelt down beside him and asked again, "Never?" Ricki was looking at me now.

His face began cooling down and he repeated, "Never." I stood and walked around his chair.

"I never listen?" I asked again. "Ricki, why didn't any of you tell me I had this, this problem?"

Ricki was bouncing again. He always bounced when he was upset or excited.

"Hello!" he sang, "You never listen." I faced him.

"What are you saying?" I asked him.

Ricki waved his left arm in the air, "I rest my case."

His arms folded and the bouncing stopped. The tears started up again and Ricki rushed to my side.

"I'm sorry I called you Ice Cream. Please don't cry again. You're low on makeup and we have a meeting today. That's what I actually came over here to tell you.

I blew my nose, "Why didn't you tell me?" I asked concerning the meeting.

He smiled and hugged me, "Because, you don't listen."

I playfully hit him and we began laughing. I held onto Ricki so tightly and he held me back. The tears didn't stop but at least I felt the comfort of a man. A man named Ricki.

Moving On

I guess about four years had passed. I toured, opening for many popular R&B artists. And, now people were opening for me. We had traveled all over the world. I was lecturing as well as doing spoken word concerts and charity work in hospitals and where ever the calls were coming from.

Everything the team touched turned into platinum. We purposely avoided the Austin, Texas area for the obvious reasons. I still saw Troy actively publicized in papers and top magazines.

Troy now had his own television talk show that was just a pulse beat away from overtaking Oprah's stats. I had to stop reading about Troy in the news once I read that he was getting married. Had I continued reading, I would have also read that he had called the wedding off and was single again.

I never dated, well not seriously. I just couldn't find anyone like Troy. No one touched my passions like he did. So many poems found a home in the memory of that passion and through those memories, the world could share and, feel just a tiny piece of what Troy and I shared. It was indeed magical, even to them. Finally, the inevitable happened. We got booked in Austin Texas.

I picked up the phone and called Toni. She and Walter had since hooked up and gotten married. And, they worked so well together.

"Hello," her voice rang on the other side of the phone.

"This is Toni. Talk to me, Austin, Texas"? Toni, I don't do Austin, Texas! You KNOW I don't do Austin!"

Toni cleared her throat, "Calm down Ren. They made us an offer we couldn't refuse."

My body was almost trembling now.

"Ok Toni," I chimed. "Since they made YOU an offer YOU couldn't refuse, YOU do Austin." With that, I hung up the phone and the tears returned.

The phone rang again and I let it. It continued ringing until I knew Toni wouldn't stop calling until I spoke to her. I picked up the phone.

"I'm not doing it." I protested. The voice on the other side of the phone was stem but understanding.

"Listen Lauren, we are all getting on that plane and you are, my Dear, going to do Austin, Texas and that's the end of it. This is your manager speaking to you. Do you hear me? Besides, what are the chances you'll see the man? And what's the big deal anyway? What's Troy got that any other man doesn't have? What, what two arms, two legs and a jimmy? I mean really what does this man have that any other man doesn't have?"

I slowly sat down as I listen to her speaking. When she became silent I answered.

"He has my heart Toni. The man has my heart." I hung up the phone and went to bed.

Toni and the others were right and I realized it. It had been four years. Four lonely years and, I was acting like it was just yesterday. I couldn't run away from Austin for the rest of my life. I had an obligation to the team. We needed to enjoy the fire while it was hot. Yes Toni, we shall go to Austin, Texas.

A week later, I found myself on the plane heading for Austin. The crew sat in first class enjoying the benefits of it all. Alexis had hooked up with her Teddy Bear and they now had four, count 'em, four kids. Teddy stayed home so she could accompany me. After all, Alexis was my personal assistant.

Alexis along with Sylvia could be heard in first class. I never flew first class. I never even liked to fly. I always said, 'if the plane crashes, first class is the first to go. At least let me have that extra split second of life...LOL. Whatever! If you go, you just go. I just decided not to go first class. That's just me.

Once we touched down, our limo took us right to our beautiful hotel. The concert was to benefit troubled youth at the Ventana Del Soul. Because of the tickets selling out, we were to perform four shows. One Friday, two on Saturday and, the final show was to be on Sunday. All sold out.

The Ventana Hotel was just beautiful. Everyone relaxed but, I spent my time alone. I wanted to be at my best. This was going to be a long vigorous weekend.

At 6:00 everyone started getting ready for the show. I always arrived at least an hour early so no one would be late. The opening act took stage at 7 sharp. I had noticed several magazines in the lobby featuring Troy. Each cover Troy was with a different woman, seemingly. I had to get it together now. It was show time.

My intro began and I glided onto the stage to the great pleasure of the crowd of fans. I waved and greeted them and began my set. It was a favorite from my second cd.

Each number got more electric and filled with love and passion. For a change, I slowed things down and performed a new piece entitled, "Then You Left Me." As I recited it and the music played softly behind my words, I could feel the audience felt every stroke of my pain. They were very quiet. I heard and felt their tears as well.

I finished the number and turned to face my band to allow the opportunity to quickly dry my own tears. Hopefully the audience didn't notice. My band members gave me an encouraging, 'you'll do fine' kind of look. The entire room was silent.

As I turned back to face them, there was a roar of approval for the new number. I smiled and my eyes moved over the sea of fans. Slowly I looked from the left and acknowledged them with a gentle wave.

My eyes scanned the crowd now slowly moving to the right. Many of them were standing, but my eyes rested on a man seated in the front row center. He was very tall and very dark and he was holding Vera Wang roses, my now favorite flowers. He was clapping vigorously. Slowly he moved towards the edge of the stage and I slowly joined him. I knelt down as he extended his arms with the flowers in them. The roar subsided as I reached out to receive the flowers.

Troy almost whispered, "Hi baby. Good to see you. You look great" I blinked back my tears and touched his with my fingertips.

"What happened?" I whispered. Troy came close enough to almost kiss me then he stopped.

"Go do your show." He said. Then turned and walked back to his seat.

I overheard someone in the audience saying to someone in the front row, "Hey man, that's Troy Johnson, the famous playwright. I'll bet that's the woman from his last novel, 'Never To Love Again.' Man I'll bet that's her!"

I smelled the fragrant flowers and passed them to Alexis who was just off the wing. "Put these in water for me please." I asked and returned to my next number.

"Okay guys!" I shouted. "Let's do this!" The crowd roared. I looked over at Troy. He was seated, silently watching.

Soon the concert was over. The lights were coming up slowly and the crowd was filing out. I was accepting flowers and well wishes from fans and shaking hands when I saw Troy rise from his seat. He was coming up on the stage towards me.

My heart was thundering. I stood, unable to move as Troy approached me. My knees were shaking and I tried so very hard to remain stable.

"How are you Troy?" I asked, my voice almost trembling. Troy didn't smile. He almost had no expression at all. Reaching out he gently took my elbow.

"Can we go somewhere and talk?" I glanced at the back stage curtain. The stage crew was motioning for everyone to clear the stage.

"Come with me to my dressing room." I answered softly.

My head was spinning now. It seemed to take forever to reach my room. Troy reached around me and opened the door. I flipped on the light and, we entered. Upon hearing the door close behind me, I spun around.

"Why did you leave me?" I asked Troy almost in tears. Troy stood there, just looking at me. "You can't imagine what you put me through Troy Johnson," still no response. "Aren't you going to say anything?" Troy reached into his coat pocket and he slowly sank to one knee.

"I never stopped loving you." Troy began almost in a whisper. "You are in my blood Lauren."

My eyes began to widen as Troy removed a small box and proceeded to open it.

"What are you doing?" I asked. The box was now open and it was....empty. I didn't speak. I just stared at the empty velvet box. Troy motioned for me to come closer. Now I was really confused. I walked closer to him. He extended his hand and pulled me gently to his knee. I found myself seated upon his knee.

"Do you see this box?" Troy asked. Then he reached into his inside pocket. In his hand was the most beautiful ring I had ever seen.

"I bought this ring four years ago right before you broke my heart". I tried to get up off his knee, but he held me.

"If you would have me, I would love to be your husband, if you would forgive me. I would love to have you as my wife."

In a very small voice I asked, "Forgive? You? Oh Troy, could you every forgive me?" Troy stood lifting me into his arms. Troy kissed me sweetly and deeply.

And then I said, "'yes".

We were married six months later and named the hottest couple in the literary world. And to think...it all began with a CONCERT...

Epilogue

I closed the book. "Wow." Was the only thought I could muster up.

"So why can't you publish this? I really enjoyed it." I watched the sadness return.

"When we had written the last chapter of this book, there was nothing else to do. At least Troy thought for us to meet. For some idiotic reason I agreed. We even made a date. You see, during the time we were writing this special crazy love story; I felt as if I were that young vivacious woman, full of life and vigor. I felt young again and life was exciting again. I felt as if Troy was taking me into his arms and loving me passionately. Then that cruel little thing called reality came tap, tap tapping at my door."

Millie reached for the manuscript and replaced it in the living room. She sank into the seat next to it.

"What would Troy think of me if he found out I wasn't 40ish or whatever age his characters love interest might be? Troy would just hate me." I noticed tears begin to trickle down Millie's cheeks.

Handing her a tissue I asked. "Are you alright Millie?" She nodded.

"I'm fine dear. There's more." I looked around for perhaps another manuscript. "No, it's not in the manuscript. You see I agreed to meet Troy at the Old Country Buffet on Mercury Boulevard. Troy was so sweet I couldn't stand him up."

I leaned forward asking, "So you met Troy then?" There was that chuckle again.

"Heavens no, child. I begged my daughter Lauren to go instead." The chuckle turned into brilliant laughter. "You should have seen her little face. It was so funny. I think Ren almost cursed." I was laughing now.

"So she went then?" Millie touched my hand.

"Lauren and I both went. It wasn't that busy during the week for breakfast. That's why we chose that time. I went in with my daughter but I never planned to stay long. We agreed that Lauren would meet this young man and maybe have a cup of coffee and then we would leave. I would sit at another table alone. No need for forcing her to do this and be a third wheel too."

I nodded my head. "I hear ya on that one Millie." Sitting back in the chair she smiled.

"Who would have known they would hit it off so well." I sat up in my seat.

"Lauren took your man?" I asked. Millie started to laugh again.

"You are silly aren't you Leigh?" I must have gotten a little carried away.

"Sorry Millie, please finish."

"Well, she, my daughter, dressed very casual and we went on in. Lauren was still protesting when we got to the Buffet. When we arrived inside there was a very handsome young man standing by the register. Oh he was so handsome. I explained to my daughter that she need not feel guilty at all. Those few days in our little fantasy land had worked miracles for me. I told her to....go for what she knew." Millie leaned back laughing.

"Is that hip still?" Millie asked. I was smiling now.

"I'm impressed Millie." I began to feel a spirit of sadness enter the atmosphere. I couldn't tell if it were coming from me or Millie. Millie continued dabbing her eyes with the tissue while still smiling.

"My daughter walked towards the register and the young man smiled, 'Lauren?' My daughter looked back at me. I could tell that she was unsure, but there was something about the expression on her beautiful face. So, I encouraged her to go on".

"I had certainly had my moment. Troy paid for their coffee and offered his arm to her. Just like Troy had done to Lauren so many times in our story. I watched them take a seat and my daughter began to glow a wonderful glow. And my, Troy looked so handsome."

I was all ears and my heart felt a tug like I've never felt before. Millie sighed and continued.

"I was thirsty so I went to the water fountain to take a sip before I left. I reached the fountain about the same time as an older gentleman reached it. The man graciously stepped back then he said the most peculiar thing." A strange expression crossed her face. Her voice trailed a bit.

"As I leaned to get a drink he said....'Nice weather we're having'. As I stood up and, he leaned to take a drink I responded, 'having weather is always nice."

I tilted my head and looked at Millie.

She continued, "I thought it was the strangest thing." I shifted in my chair.

"Then what happened?" Millie rose and walked to the kitchen.

"I left. My daughter, however, is still seeing this young man. Thank goodness she's a writer. They come to visit me often and, I adore him. It makes my heart glad to see them together like that. They're getting married next month."

I didn't know what to say. That was kind of weird, her daughter marrying her man. But it really wasn't her man. It was a fantasy life she had going on the internet. Wow! And, now she was alone again. That was messed up. But, at least Millie was writing again. Too bad she couldn't get that manuscript published.

Millie told me her daughter and her fiancé were due to come over so, I figured I had stayed long enough. I wanted to be gone before they both arrived, but they came early.

The knock, although halfway expecting it, still startled me. I gathered my recorder. I had my story and, a very interesting one at that.

"Well, Millie, that's my cue to jet." Millie rushed past me to answer the door.

"Oh no Leigh, you must meet my daughter Lauren!" She opened the door and indeed her daughter was quite beautiful and, the young man who accompanied her was very handsome.

Millie let them both in and promptly introduced us. I shook their hands as Millie began to close the door. The young man, Troy protested.

"My father is going to be joining us. I introduced Lauren to him and we were both surprised that you two live in the same building. My dad moved in here last week! For some odd reason he suddenly decided he wanted his independence." It wasn't long before an older gentleman accompanied by a woman entered the room.

"Mom, this is Troy's father...his name is Troy Sr." Millie's daughter proudly introduced us.

The woman whom I believed to be his wife, turned out to be his sister. Troy's father was equally handsome even at his age. You could see that he was truly a looker in his day.

"Haven't I seen you somewhere before?" Troy Sr., asked Millie. She smiled and shook her head no. She embraced her daughter and her son in law to be.

"Now I must leave" I insisted.

It was getting a little crowded for me in that small apartment. How sad I thought, that Millie was not able to have the man of her dreams be the man of her dreams.

"Please don't leave now." Lauren requested. "We're going out and we would love to have you come along."

Perhaps Lauren was just being polite. I was going, my mind was made up.

As Millie accompanied me to the door again, I thanked her for her time and hospitality. Suddenly we heard Troy Sr., call out.

"Oh my goodness!"

We turned to see what the commotion was all about. He was holding the manuscript.

"Where did you get this?" Troy Sr. asked. Millie quickly moved towards Troy Sr., and reached for the manuscript.

"That's mine, I wrote it." she insisted. An expression of delight crossed Troy Sr.'s face.

"And so did I!" he chimed. Smiling he asked, "Ren?"

Millie smiled, "Troy?"

They both answered in unison, "YES!!"

They embraced like two long lost lovers. I'll just be ham boned! It was dude from the story. And now living right up stairs! How cool is that?

"Now you must stay," Millie insisted.

And so, stay I guess I must. There was certainly more of this story to get and I was going to get it.

Later on they actually did publish this story. It's currently on the best sellers list and to beat all, I'm sitting here watching the screen play. How about that?

I guess having weather IS always nice.

Here, have some popcorn.

END?

The Story Behind The Story

I shared with you all how this book came about. What I didn't tell you was the simple attention getter that sparked this artistic friendship. It was a simple poem about Ice Cream. That's right Ice......Cream.

Anyone who knows me and I mean "Really" knows me understands my relationship with ice cream. I was about fed up with the men on BP hitting me up with crazy lines and scams and the like. I was in a relationship so I wasn't looking to find another man. One at a time suits me just fine. I was working on some promotions material when he hit me up. Then this poem came across my screen:

A Poem about an ice cream cone.
Posted 8/20/08

First Time

It was Boston, Logan,
You were sitting there,
Eating an ice cream cone,
Shoes off.
Feet up.
I watched you from afar,
You were confident in your look,
Or either didn't care,
Hair cut short
Tailored suit,

Expensive shoes cast aside.
Focusing on the ice cream cone,

Your tongue caressed the sweetness,
Your mouth accepted it graciously,
Your eyes slid back in pleasure.
Your lips surrounded the creamy ooze,

The redness of your lips,
Against the whiteness of the cream,
Droplets in the corner of your mouth,
Tongue darting to prevent the escapees.
Your hand was wrapped around the cone,
You held it with tender care,
Your fingertips caressing the ridges,
While inhaling the aroma of the cream.

Then your tongue flicked around the cone,
Catching the melting ooze,
Retrieving it for your waiting mouth,
Swallowing it sensuously and smiling.
Toes curled as your tongue encircled the cone,
You sucked the cream as you crossed your legs,
I thought I heard a moan of delight,
As you touched your lips to the tip.

Your appetite grew and you opened your mouth,
Inserted the cone into your mouth,
You squeezed the sides of the confection,
And it gave up the prize.
This was the first time,
I saw you.

©The Ebony Poet

My first thought was, "Wow" as I began to taste this cool creamy treat. I asked him how he knew I loved ice cream. I could feel him smile through the key strokes. Then our conversation shifted to Anita as he inquired about my being there on the planet. The rest is history.

Memory

My heart beats for you
an alluring melody.
Taking me by surprise,
I loved you
on
purpose.

The memory of your eyes
burned swiftly through
my soul
and the sounds
surrounded.....
me

I didn't want for you to go
I didn't mean for you to go
I didn't need for you to go
but yet .....
you left me.

And now lying in my bed
with your memory in my head
all my thoughts through
tear drops shed.......
I'm so empty.

Daylight brings a brilliant sun
kissing me upon my face
the warmth is wonderful
but it isn't you.
As the dew engulfs the ground
more tears within my soul are found

In my longingness of longing
there's only you.

I didn't want for you to go
I didn't mean for you to go
I didn't need for you to go
but yet you left me

And now staring at the phone
wondering if you're at home
I hunger for all things
that equal
we.

My soul calls to you
an unmistakable symphony
I reach for you
cos you loved me
on
purpose

My heart reaches
for the phone
Screaming softly
"I'm so alone"
And hearing your voice
it whispers
"Please forgive
me"

©Psoemetry June 2001

About the Authors

The Ebony Poet

The Ebony Poet is the pen name for a writer whose passion is poetry. He has written and self-published several chapbooks that are available via lulu.com and in local bookstores. He excels in romantic erotica and enjoys sharing his work with others.

He is a native of Arkansas, spent most of his adult life in NY and now resides in Texas with his family. The poet was educated with the public school system of Arkansas and graduated from a HBCU in Arkansas with graduate studies at SUNY Binghamton, NY; University of Texas and Northeastern University.

Psoemetry

Born January 9, 1954 this comically unique individual has been on one mission and one mission only; the great adventure called LIFE. It began in a military hospital in Fort Campbell Kentucky and the Great Adventure has never stopped.

A writer almost from birth, the first award was presented while attending Warwick High School in Newport News, Virginia. Psoemetry's talents became noticed by a special media arts teacher while holding down a spot on the High School Radio Show. The show was only 15 min a week but it wasn't long before Psoemetry owned 5 of those 15 minutes with her first Radio Show spot entitled "Getting to Know You" She was awarded "The Quill And Scroll" Award for media excellence.

Being a fan of Nicci Giovanni and Mya Angelo, her creative juices kicked into high gear as she experimented with music and high emotion. Psoemetry saved up her pennies to purchase a double tape recorder and a synthesizer laying the foundation for a very interesting future in music and spoken word.

Believe it or not the launching pad was a platform in Church. Psoemetry gave her life to Christ in 1980 and actually began reciting poetry during testimonial service. Her work was so well received; she began getting invitations from various churches in Tacoma Washington to share poetry on a more public level. This opened doors for "The Good News Poets" and many one woman poetry shows for the Poetress.

It wasn't until 2008 that the spoken word art kicked in. With a desire to submit lyrics to Ms Anita Baker, Psoemetry along with her youngest son, began putting more romantic laced pieces together backed by original music composed by her son Ben Sedgwick and his partner Sara Gibson on B$G Entertainment. As the project progressed, Psoemetry also began co-producing some of the music for this sample that soon turned into a full CD titled Sweet Surrender. It was jointly agreed to go ahead and launch this work. The original artist name selected was The Quiett Storme. (Of soft spoken word for the grown and sexy) But with tons of spoken word artists with this name, it was later decided that the new name would become Psoemetry. The worse piece on the CD was submitted to Taxi Music for a review and it was a joy to find that the least piece received a 7 out of 10 rating.

Psoemetry met Chakezulu, a homeless advocate on myspace.com prior to the making of Sweet Surrender. He inspired Psoemetry to become an artist voice for the less fortunate citizens.....the street people. This prompted the writing of *Don't Forget About Me* (the first video project taken on by the artist.) Psoemetry, along with Clyde Anderson of Andy Clyde's Inc, took to the streets of Atlanta the day after Christmas in 2007 and filmed life on the streets of Atlanta. Benjamin Sedgwick produced the film. This touching video was placed on YouTube and secured the artist with a listing in the Cambridge Who's Who in 2009.

Today Psoemetry continues to write and perform her unique pieces bringing laughter, smiles and much love to the listeners. She spends much of her spare time with her family being inspired and encouraged. A single parent of 7 (4 adult sons and 3 teen age daughters) there is much inspiration to be had. Keep an eye open for much more from this artist/writer. You can enjoy samples of her work at **http://psoemetry.com**. You can also purchase additional work there. Her upcoming project is *"The Love Of Psoemetry"* coming in the very near future.

-The Millionaire Konnection PR-2011

<u>Works Of Psoemetry</u>

Books of Poetry to include pieces published in 3 Anthologies:

Children's books - *The Granny Good's Favorite Bedtime Series*

Articles in the *Tacoma Facts* News Paper

Co Host on Christian Radio Show -*Taking It To The Streets*

Spoken Word CD - *Sweet Surrender*

Where To Find Psoemetry:

http://psoemetry.com

www.reverbnation.com/thequiettstorme

www.twitter.com/sandrasedgwickw

www.psoemetry.blogspot.com

www.myspace.com/ourquietstorm

www.jango.com/music/Psoemetry

www.ingramcontent.com/pod-product-compliance
Lightning Source LLC
Chambersburg PA
CBHW060625130626
46555CB00002B/665